THE MEASURE OF A HEART

Books by Janette Oke

Another Homecoming*
Celebrating the Inner Beauty of Woman
Janette Oke's Reflections on the Christmas Story
The Matchmakers
Nana's Gift
The Red Geranium
Return to Harmony*
Spunky's First Christmas
Tomorrow's Dream*

CANADIAN WEST

When Calls the Heart   When Breaks the Dawn
When Comes the Spring   When Hope Springs New

LOVE COMES SOFTLY

Love Comes Softly   Love's Unending Legacy
Love's Enduring Promise   Love's Unfolding Dream
Love's Long Journey   Love Takes Wing
Love's Abiding Joy   Love Finds a Home

A PRAIRIE LEGACY

The Tender Years

SEASONS OF THE HEART

Once Upon a Summer   Winter Is Not Forever
The Winds of Autumn   Spring's Gentle Promise

WOMEN OF THE WEST

The Calling of Emily Evans   A Bride for Donnigan
Julia's Last Hope   Heart of the Wilderness
Roses for Mama   Too Long a Stranger
A Woman Named Damaris   The Bluebird and the Sparrow
They Called Her Mrs. Doc   A Gown of Spanish Lace
The Measure of a Heart   Drums of Change

DEVOTIONALS

The Father Who Calls   Father of My Heart
The Father of Love   Faithful Father

———

Janette Oke: A Heart for the Prairie
Biography of Janette Oke by Laurel Oke Logan

*with T. Davis Bunn

9801

JANETTE OKE

THE MEASURE OF A HEART

BETHANY HOUSE PUBLISHERS
MINNEAPOLIS, MINNESOTA 55438

The Measure of a Heart
Copyright © 1992
Janette Oke

Cover by Dan Thornberg,
Bethany House Publishers staff artist.

Published by Bethany House Publishers
A Ministry of Bethany Fellowship International
11300 Hampshire Avenue South
Minneapolis, Minnesota 55438

Printed in the United States of America by
Bethany Press International
Minneapolis, Minnesota 55438

Library of Congress Catalog Number 92–547
ISBN 1–55661–296–6 (Trade Paper Edition)
ISBN 1–55661–297–4 (Large Print Edition)
ISBN 0–7642–2100–0 (Mass Market Edition)

I have been privileged to be a part of a large and loving family. Many aunts and uncles have each added something "special" to my life, both when I was a child and later as an adult. There is so much I would like to share about each one of them. Since space will not allow that, I wish to pay tribute to my Ruggles heritage by dedicating this book with my love and thanks to:

Uncle Royal and Aunt Bea
Uncle Burt
Aunt Laurine
Uncle Wayne and Aunt Violet
Uncle Bob
Aunt Jean and Jim
Uncle Harry and Aunt Marion

Thank you all for your love

And in loving memory of wonderful aunts and uncles who have already gathered with Jesus:

Aunt Carrie, Uncle Jack, Aunt Leone and Uncle Walter, Uncle Ross and Aunt Hazel, Aunt Marie, and Uncle Dorn.

JANETTE OKE was born in Champion, Alberta, during the depression years, to a Canadian prairie farmer and his wife. She is a graduate of Mountain View Bible College in Didsbury, Alberta, where she met her husband, Edward. They were married in May of 1957, and went on to pastor churches in Indiana as well as Calgary and Edmonton, Canada.

The Okes have three sons and one daughter and are enjoying the addition of grandchildren to the family. Edward and Janette have both been active in their local church, serving in various capacities as Sunday school teachers and board members. They make their home near Calgary, Alberta.

Contents

Chapter One

Anna

The rays of the late afternoon sun poured down upon her head, splashed over and spilled onto the thin blue calico that covered her slender shoulders. She had pushed her bonnet back and loosed the braids that usually held her hair captive, running her fingers through the heavy brown locks so they fell about her, thick and wavy, making her face seem almost pixyish.

But she paid no attention to the warmth of the sun, nor to the tresses that wisped about her face. Her thoughts far away, she did not notice the sounds or stirring around her. Her bare feet dragged listlessly through the dust of the rutted track that the locals referred to as the Main Road. But even though part of her was deep in thought, her intense blue eyes scanned the grasses at the sides of the road, alert to small groupings of red that announced wild strawberries tucked among the greenery.

Her worn school shoes, the only ones she owned, were tied together by frayed laces and hung loosely from her shoulder. They swayed lightly as she walked, but she did not pay them notice either. Only when she stopped and bent over did she even remember they were there. Then she held them in place by pressing an elbow against the one that hung in front while her hands reached out to pluck the sweet berries. She deposited them carefully in the red metal lunch pail with the scratched-in initials A.T. for Anna Trent.

She could have eaten the berries—but even in her state of distraction, she automatically placed them in the small container, conscious of the small hands that would reach eagerly for them when she arrived home.

Her thoughts were not on the warm day, nor the dust at her feet, nor even the berries that she placed carefully in the small pail. They were more seriously occupied. This was her last day of school. Her last day ever! And she would miss it. Would miss it terribly.

But even as the sad thoughts filled her being and tightened her throat with unshed tears, she knew she had been blessed. Why, most of the girls her age had been forced long ago to drop out to help at home. Here she was, already past her sixteenth birthday, and still trudging off to school with the little kids. Oh, not every day. In fact, she had missed almost a solid year when her mama had been so ill. And there were the seed times, the harvests, the days when Mama just couldn't do without her help. But she had gone enough to easily keep up with her classmates. But not any longer. She had completed the eighth grade. There wasn't any more school for her.

Quite suddenly she broke from her reverie and lifted her eyes to the afternoon sky. A shocked look crossed her face when she saw where the sun was.

My, she'd been dawdling. She hadn't realized. Her mama would wonder what on earth had become of her.

She straightened from her crouched position and let the handful of ripe berries trickle from her stained fingers. She had to get home. There was work to be done before the sun set and the farmhouse door closed against the spring darkness.

Her bare feet slapped the earth with rapid regularity, causing the dust to lift with each step, swirling around her and clinging to the hem of her calico skirts. Every now and then she reached down to shake her skirt of the encroaching dust—but she could not shake her thoughts as easily. *School is over. Finished. I'll never go again* hung heavily upon her, clinging to every awareness of her quick and active mind.

She had loved school. Had been an apt student. Could have accomplished great things had she had the opportunity. She did not think about that. But her teachers had. Anna only knew that she loved to learn, loved the excitement of new discoveries, loved the quickening of her pulse as she shared some great adventure in the pages of a book. Through books, her mind—her life—was made to stretch and grow and become more aware of the world about her and beyond her.

And now that was over. She had reached the end of the road. The last day of the eighth grade.

With one final swish of her skirts, she turned the corner into her own farmyard and proceeded with quick steps toward the house. Mama would be tired from her long day. Anna dreaded the first glimpse of the pale face, the listless eyes, the drooping shoulders that marked another day at the laundry tubs or the long rows of spring vegetables. Her mama worked so hard—and she, Anna, had dawdled over tiny wild strawberries.

She entered the kitchen and placed her pail on the small table by the door. Her mama was at the cupboard, her back turned, and yes, her shoulders were drooping; but at the sound of stirring behind her, she turned. Anna was tempted to lower her gaze so she wouldn't see the tiredness in the eyes, but she could not. Clear blue eyes met smoky gray ones. Anna saw the weariness she had expected, but she also saw the gray eyes lighten quickly, a warmth and eagerness making them brighten.

"You got your eighth-grade certificate?" her mama asked, excitement filling her voice and spilling over into her face.

Anna's eyes shone in turn. She nodded her head and reached to the bodice of her dress where she had carefully tucked the certificate so she wouldn't stain it with berry juices. She eased out the slight crease in the paper and handed it to her mother.

"Grade eight!" the woman exclaimed as her eyes fell to the small but important document.

Her eyes sparkled with unshed tears as she carefully studied it.

"It says I finished the eighth grade with first-class honors," said Anna, almost under her breath. She hated to boast, but she knew her mama might not be able to read all the words.

"First-class honors," repeated the woman. "I'm so proud," and she reached out a calloused hand and let it rest on the wavy brown hair. "So proud t' have an edjicated daughter."

The tears did fall then, and the woman laid the bit of paper on the nearby table, brushed her cheeks with the hem of her flour-sack apron, then moved back toward the cupboards.

"Sorry I'm so late," Anna apologized. "I got picking strawberries and lost track of the time."

"Isn't every day that a girl graduates," excused her mother, running her rolling pin over the crust for a pie. "I got the last of the apples up from the root cellar," she said. "Getting kind of wrinkled and scrawny. Figured they had to be used up. You pare 'em before you peel the supper potatoes. The boys are out doing up the chores. Pa is in the east field. I'm sure he'll work until it's dark. He's so anxious to get that crop in—with the rainy weather puttin' him way behind. 'Course he's further ahead than some of the neighbors. Mr. Rubens ain't half done, and Ole Hank hardly has him a start. But then he don't have much help. Just has them girls, and they are none too ambitious—and them not even going t' school much since sixth grade." She raised her head a moment to look again at Anna. "Eighth grade. Just think of it. I'm so proud to have a daughter so edjicated!"

Anna was used to her mother's chatter. Used to the run-on topics that seemed disconnected and yet were all woven together by some unknown thread of thought. She knew how much her mother needed someone to talk to. Stuck at home with all the household chores, with two small boys still clinging to her skirts, with rowdy school sons tumbling in and out of her kitchen for the remainder of her day. With a husband either in the fields or in the barns. She needed *someone* to talk to. And Anna was her only girl. Her only companion. One girl with six younger brothers. No wonder her mother talked nonstop when Anna arrived home from school.

"I'd better change," Anna managed to fit in when her mother stopped for a breath, and the older woman nodded, the rolling pin working smoothly back and forth under her expert hands.

Anna moved quickly to the little room at the back of the kitchen. It was small and simple, but neat and private. Her little place of solitude—her sanctuary. She wished she could stay there now—tuck herself among the pillows on her bed and pick up one of her worn books, or just bury her head in the pillow and have herself a good cry.

She didn't understand why she felt like crying—she with her education, she who had been so singularly blessed. But she felt weepy nonetheless.

She didn't stop to indulge herself, though. Her mother needed her in the kitchen. She slipped the calico over her head and hung it properly on its peg. Then her hand reached for the simple brown garment that was her household chore dress. She let it fall over her slim shoulders and settle about her. The brown dress seemed to smother her small frame. She didn't like the dress. It always made her look and feel like a small child lost in brown straw.

I'm so—so skinny, she thought to herself for the hundredth time. She made a face at her own reflection in the piece of mirror that hung on her wall. *So shiny and—plain.* Her thoughts continued.

Small face, skinny cheeks, little bit of a chin, thin lips—only my nose is big, too big for the rest of me. I wish my face was bigger—or my nose smaller. Something—something to balance me off. And I look all lost in all this—this sack of a dress, this hair.

Her eyes lifted again to the mirror. She really did look lost, she concluded, as her blue eyes stared back at her. They looked too big for the small, thin face. Anna flung her hair back from her face and turned away from the mirror in discouragement. Then she reached for a piece of ribbon and quickly bound the hair back at the nape of her neck.

With one last disdainful glance at her own reflection, she left the room and hurried out to help her mother in the kitchen.

Her mother was already speaking when she entered the room.

"As soon as you finish the apples and peelin' the supper potatoes, the milk and cream have t' go to the parson's. She might be needin' it for her supper."

Anna nodded and moved quickly to tie a large apron over the large brown dress. She had an added incentive to hurry with the peeling now. She loved the short walk to the parsonage. And she loved her little chats with the kind Mrs. Angus or her elderly pastor husband. Here were people who were *really* educated—and Anna had so much she longed to learn.

Chapter Two

Surprise

Anna hurried down the road with the pails of milk. Even though she hadn't been to the parsonage for a while, she knew she would not have long to visit on this night. The supper potatoes were already put on to boil, the withered-apple pies placed in the cooking ovens. Her mama would need her back quickly to set the table and help with the dishing up.

No, this time she wouldn't get to linger and chat at the parsonage. Still, she had tucked her eighth-grade certificate in the large pocket in her apron—it wouldn't do to dig in the bodice of her brown dress in order to show it to the minister and his wife. But she was concerned that one of the heavy pails might bump up against it and wrinkle the smooth parchment. Her arms ached as she walked carefully, trying to hurry, yet hold the pails slightly away from her body.

She should have left the certificate at home, she chided herself. She would likely go and spoil it—and she'd never have a chance to get another one.

But Mrs. Angus had made her promise that she'd bring the important piece of paper and show it to her. Anna was both a bit proud and a little embarrassed to be toting around the proof of her accomplishment, but she would never have considered trying to wriggle out of a promise.

So she walked awkwardly—hurriedly—in spite of her discomfort. The pails were heavy enough anyway, but doubly so with the difficult way in which she was carrying them.

She had to stop every now and then to rest her tired arms. That cut into her precious minutes. She would be so glad to exchange the heavy full pails for returned empties.

At last Anna reached the boardwalk that led to the back door of the small parsonage. She was flushed and out of breath as she hastened down the clattering boards, set her pail carefully at her feet, and lifted an aching arm to knock on the door. One hand traced the outline of her precious certificate in the apron pocket. She fervently hoped that she hadn't wrinkled it, but she could hardly take it out to check lest she be caught with it in her hand. That would appear far too boastful, she was sure.

She sighed a bit impatiently. She knew it often took the elderly woman a few minutes to make her way to the door. She had arthritis in one hip and moved very slowly with her "hobblin' stick," as Anna's small brother Karl called the cane. Sometimes the pastor himself opened the door. Then Anna did not have to wait quite as long for a response to her knock. Either way, she always felt welcomed and accepted at the parsonage. She loved to come. But tonight her stay could not be long. She hated every ticking second that cut back on her time.

And then she heard footsteps approaching the door. Her heart quickened and a smile lit her eyes and gently curved her lips. *It is not Mrs. Angus,* Anna was thinking, realizing that the steps were moving quickly and lightly across the kitchen floor with no accompanying thump of the cane. But neither did it sound like—

The door opened and a stranger stood with his hand on the doorknob. Anna's smile quickly faded and she blinked in confusion.

"I'm—I'm sorry," she began to stammer, taking a step backward. But the man was smiling and motioning for her to enter the kitchen.

Anna held back. She had never seen him before. She knew he was not from their small town—their community.

"You're the young Trent girl," he was saying, the smile still on his face. "Mrs. Angus told me you'd be bringing milk." He placed a hand lightly on the sleeve of her brown cotton and gently urged her into the room. Anna still did not budge.

"Where is Mrs. Angus?" she finally managed. She wished she could still the beating of her heart. Had something dreadful happened? Was Mrs. Angus ill? Who was this—this stranger?

"The Anguses are taking a few weeks off," he said matter-of-factly. "I've been sent to fill in for the summer months."

Anna didn't respond, just reached down to lift her heavy pails of milk and move woodenly through the door. She intended to deposit them on the small table against the far wall. She could see the clean, empty pails awaiting her. She wouldn't need time for a visit after all. Wouldn't need the certificate that now seemed to hang heavily in her apron pocket.

But he gently eased the pails from her fingers. His eyebrows lifted slightly. "These are heavy," he observed and Anna nodded her head dumbly.

"Your name is Anna?" he asked, lifting the pails onto the table.

Anna nodded her head again, forgetting that his back was turned to her and that he could not see her response.

He turned to face her and asked again, handing her the two empty pails, "You're Anna?"

"Yes," she managed.

"Mrs. Angus was fretting. She hated to leave before you arrived. Said that she wanted to see your school—something-or-other."

"Certificate," Anna filled in and had to stop to swallow. "My eighth-grade certificate."

She felt so silly standing there before this man, talking about eighth grade.

"Did you bring it?" he asked with seeming interest.

Anna managed to lift her eyes to his.

"Yes," she answered simply.

"May I see it?"

He reached out a hand and Anna fumbled in her apron pocket, certainly thankful that she had not put the certificate in the bodice of her brown cotton.

She produced the piece of paper, relieved when she saw that it had not been damaged by the jostling of the pails. She wasn't sure, though, if she wished to turn it over to a total stranger. Reluctantly she released her hold when his hand reached out to take the paper from her. He studied it carefully, his eyes showing pleasure as he read.

"With first-class honors," he read softly. "That's

commendable. Mrs. Angus will be very pleased."

His eyes found hers again and Anna felt her face flushing.

"I'm planning to write them with a weekly report," he told her. "Do you mind if I share the news with her?"

Anna managed to find her tongue. "How long will they be gone?"

"Only for the summer." He handed her back her precious certificate, and she quickly pushed it into her pocket. He went on, "A granddaughter is getting married—then they are to take a bit of rest. They'll be back again when I head back to school this fall."

Anna looked at him, her eyes growing wider. Why, he must be well past twenty, and here he was still going to school! Boys—men—could be so fortunate.

She wished she could ask him about his school but the words stuck in her throat. She wondered what he was studying—how much longer he could go on with schooling. Oh, if only she were allowed to go on to school—to study. There was so much she didn't know. She wondered just how long a person would need to go to school before he had learned everything there was to learn.

Her thoughts whirled through her mind and she shifted uncomfortably. Then she noticed the kitchen table where Mrs. Angus always had an African violet, usually with blooms. The pastor's wife rotated them from creamy white to shades of pink or blue or purple. Mrs. Angus loved her violets. To Anna's surprise, the table was now stacked and strewn with books of varying sizes. Her eyes widened again. He seemed to notice.

"Commentaries," he explained simply. "I have to keep studying—even if I am out of class for the summer. Right now I'm working on Sunday's sermon."

Anna was unable to respond.

"Have you ever seen a Bible commentary?" he was asking, moving slowly toward the table.

"No," admitted Anna, her head shaking as her brow furrowed slightly.

"Well, they are books filled with explanations about the Scriptures. They also expand on the stories, give insight into the culture of the people. So that you can understand the meanings of sayings or situations."

He reached for the nearest book and began to flip the pages. Anna saw pictures tucked among the many words. She yearned to hold the book in her own hands.

"Do you like Bible stories?" he was asking.

"Oh yes," she whispered.

"Mrs. Angus says that you have a very good mind—are eager to learn. That was why she was so anxious to see your school report. By the look of it, she was right. Honors! That's good." He smiled encouragingly at her.

"Actually, the most important learning we can ever do," he went on, "is to learn the Word of God. That's why I am going to seminary. To learn God's Word."

Anna felt envy wash over her whole being, then quickly rebuked herself.

"I'm through," the thought spilled out verbally. "I'm all done at school now."

"With school—maybe. But not with learning. We never need to quit learning," said the young man, nodding his head at the pile of books. "I don't plan to quit learning when I have finished seminary. In fact, my learning will have just begun. There is so much more I need to know. Seminary just shows me how to go about finding knowledge."

The blue of Anna's eyes intensified. Was there no end to what one could learn? She felt dwarfed—bereft. She was so limited.

"Would you like to borrow a book?" the man was asking.

Anna could only stare. Had she heard him right? Was he actually offering her one of those wonderful volumes?

She longed to reach out and claim the treasure, but she shrank back slightly.

"Would you?" he prompted.

"Oh, I—I couldn't," she managed to murmur.

"Why not? Won't you have time to read?"

"Oh yes. Mama always gives me time when I have a book. In—in fact, they usually have me read the book aloud—to the whole family, but—"

"Then you need a book. Oh, not one of these commentaries but . . . let's see." He crossed to the shelf behind him and began to scan the titles.

Anna could only stare. She had never seen so many books all in one place before except at the schoolhouse. This young man was blessed indeed. First of all, to still be able to go to school. Secondly, to have so many, many books at his fingertips, so much knowledge right at hand.

He chose a book and turned to hold it out to her. "This should be a good one," he was saying. "I think you and your family will enjoy—"

But Anna could not lift her hand to accept the book. She shook her head again and swallowed with difficulty. "What—what if something happened to it?" she managed at last.

He smiled. It made his whole face light up. "Mrs. Angus would not have spoken so highly of you if you were not to be trusted," he answered.

"But—" began Anna.

"I know. Even trustworthy people can have accidents. But should you—in spite of your carefulness—then the book can be replaced. Please. Read it. Share it with your family. That's what books are for."

Anna could no longer resist. She reached for the book, swallowed again, thinking of the seriousness of trust placed in her. "I will—will be most careful," she promised solemnly as the volume came into her possession.

"I know you will." He smiled again.

Then Anna realized that she had taken far more time than she had intended. She backed slowly toward the door. She'd have to run all the way home.

"Thank you," she muttered, then raised her voice slightly to repeat the words again, "Thank you . . . very much." Her voice was trembling with excitement and she clutched the book to her bosom.

"When you finish that one, you can exchange it for another," he promised and he was smiling again.

She answered his smile shyly and turned to go.

"Anna," he called after her. "You didn't say if I could tell Mrs. Angus about your grade report."

Anna turned long enough to nod in agreement, and then she was through the door and out on the board sidewalk. She dared not run yet. He would hear the pounding of her feet. Not till she was out on the dirt road.

But she could hardly wait. More than a need to hurry pressed her forward. Now excitement made it hard for her to keep her steps in check. It would not be difficult at all to run all the way home.

❧   ❧   ❧

"Guess what?" she cried before she was even in the kitchen. "Guess what, Mama?"

Her mother turned from the cupboard where she was slicing thick pieces of homemade bread, her eyes wide at the uncharacteristic excitement in the voice of her only daughter.

"I've got a book!" Anna exclaimed joyously.

"A book?"

"He gave me a book. Said we could all read it together. And when we are done with this one—we can go get another one!" She was so out of breath that she could scarcely get out the words.

"What are you talking about, child?" asked her mother, sounding perplexed at Anna's outburst.

Anna held up the book for her mother to see. "This!" she exclaimed. "He gave me this."

"Who? What he?"

Anna's hurried thoughts slid to a stop. So much had happened. Where should she begin?

"The new minister," she replied.

"What new minister?"

"The one who came to take the place of Anguses."

The older woman clutched at a corner of her

apron in shock. "Mercy me!" she exclaimed. "Has something happened to that poor woman?"

Anna was quick to explain. "No, she's fine. Gone to a granddaughter's wedding. But then they are taking some time to rest. Will be gone for the summer. Then they'll be back, he said."

"And just who is this 'he' you're goin' on about? What're you talking about, child?"

"The new minister. Oh, he's not a minister really. He said that he is still going to school—but he—"

"To school? You mean they sent us a boy?"

"He's not a boy," Anna argued. "He's a grown man."

"Still schoolin'?" Mrs. Trent swished her apron. Doubt edged her voice and made her eyes dark. "Must be awful slow if he's a man and still—"

But Anna's impatience cut in. "He *is* a man," she maintained, "and he's not slow. I could tell by his talking. He's going to a special school—to learn about God's Word. He said so. Said there was more to learn than he'll ever know. It's—it's called—a semintary."

"A cemetery's where ya bury folks," her mother informed her.

"Well, it's something like that—but it's a school. He said so."

Mrs. Trent turned back to her cutting board. "Well, put up your book, wash your hands, and set the table. We're soon gonna have a stampede of hungry folks stompin' into this kitchen and supper ain't on."

Anna ran to her bedroom to put away the precious book, then hurried back to wash her hands at the corner basin. She knew there was work to be done. She knew it would be several hours before the supper dishes were clean and placed back on the shelves. But oh, how she longed to open the pages of the book and discover just what the young man had given her.

"Who is this young fella?" her mother was asking again.

"A . . . a summer replacement," Anna answered lamely. "Just a summer replacement for the Anguses."

"Where's he from?"

"He didn't say," said Anna, crossing the room to lift a stack of plates from the kitchen shelf.

Her mother moved back to the stove and turned the frying slices of meat in the large iron skillet.

"What's his name?"

"He didn't say that either," admitted Anna and her mother looked up in surprise. Anna knew that if it had been her mother delivering the milk, she would have garnered a great deal more information about the new preacher.

"What's he like?" asked her mother suddenly.

Anna stopped in her tracks. What was he like? She didn't really know. Her eyes had been too intent on studying the covers of the books. How could she answer her mother?

"What do you mean?" she responded, stalling for time.

"What's he like? Tall? Short? Pleasant? Sour? What's he like?"

Anna felt she could make some observations that might satisfy her mother. "Well, he's—he's pleasant." That much was safe. Hadn't he given her a book? "And—he—he's about Papa's height." She hoped that was close.

"What's he look like?"

Anna strained to remember. She couldn't recall one more feature. And then it came to her. "Well, he—he smiles—nicely," she replied and hoped with all her heart that it would suffice.

But her mother still went on. "How old?" she asked.

Anna looked at the unusual expression on the familiar face before her. What an odd question— even from her mother.

"I don't know," she mumbled, placing another plate on the table. "Mid-twenties, I expect." She hesitated, wondering just which track her mother's thoughts were following. "But he seems knowledge-able enough," she hastened to add.

She did not see the lift of her mother's chin or the slight cocking of her head as she carefully stud-ied her daughter for one brief minute; then the woman nodded and a smile played about the cor-ners of her mouth.

Chapter Three

Learning

"Well—he can preach," announced Mrs. Trent as she pulled the pins from her Sunday bonnet.

Mr. Trent nodded his head in agreement and raised both hands to release his neck from the confines of his Sunday collar and tie.

Anna said nothing. She was still studying the cover of the new book. The family had not yet finished the last one, but the young man had offered her a second one anyway.

"Barker. That will make a nice name for a parson," Mrs. Trent commented. "I wonder what his first name is."

"Austin," put in Adam, Anna's fourteen-year-old brother as he snitched a raw carrot from the cooking pot on the cupboard. "He told me."

"Pastor Austin Barker," repeated Mrs. Trent and nodded her head as though giving her approval.

Anna went to her room to change from her Sunday dress and release her hair from its tight braids.

"Adam! Stay out of dinner until it's cooked," she heard her mother scolding. "Wouldn't be much left if all the family took from the pot."

As she gently closed her door, Anna agreed that

it had been a good sermon. She had sat forward on the bench as she listened. *Where did one get all that knowledge? Was this what going on to school could do for you?*

He had described the desert of Sinai just as though he had been there himself. And when he spoke of Moses and his struggles with the faltering new nation coming forth from the slavery of Egypt, it was so real Anna could almost feel the sting of the desert sand and the dryness of a parched throat. No wonder they had begged for water. No wonder their patience had been thin. And maybe no wonder that God had been patient with them.

Anna sat on her bed and stared at the book she held in her hands, wondering what wonderful secrets it might share with her. She wished she could curl up on her bed and start reading it immediately. But her mother was awaiting her help with the Sunday dinner. With a sigh, Anna laid aside the book and slipped out of her Sunday frock.

She reached for her calico dress. She could wear it now for everyday. She wouldn't be needing it for school anymore. She might as well get all the wear from it that she could before she grew out of it—if she ever did decide to grow. She was sure she wasn't much bigger than she had been at thirteen. She sighed again and tied her sash at the back. She did wish that she was taller—fuller. She looked like a child when she was with girls her own age.

When she returned to the kitchen, her father was trying to hustle the six boys out from under her mother's feet.

"Out on the back porch—all of ya," he said, waving a hand toward the door.

Young Karl, four, began to complain. "I'm hungry," he insisted.

"An' yer ma will get dinner on twice as fast if she doesn't have to trip over you," Mr. Trent insisted as he swung the youngest, one-and-a-half-year-old Petey, up into his arms.

The kitchen was soon cleared of all but Anna and her mother, and without a word to each other they went about the dinner preparations.

"What did you think of him?" her mother asked suddenly.

Anna's head came up. "Of what—who?" she queried.

"The young parson."

"He's—he's not a parson yet," Anna reminded her. "He said he still has two more years of schooling."

Once again Anna envied him those two more years.

"Well—he will be a parson soon enough. Two years goes by awful fast. Why, in two years you'll be eighteen."

Anna wondered briefly what that had to do with anything. Then her thoughts quickly turned to the two months the young man was to be with them. Two months. Only two months to learn all she could from his stack of books. Such a short time—and so much to learn.

Anna hurried with the setting of the table, anxious to get dinner over, the dishes done, so she might be able to sneak off to her secret rock by the creek and read until she was needed to help with supper.

"Well. . . ? What did you think?"

Again Anna had to jerk her attention back to her mother and try to remember to what she was referring. Oh yes, the young minister. But what was the question?

"He—he preaches—fine," she managed. "I—I liked the story the way he told it."

Her mother nodded. "Told yer pa he was a fine preacher," she went on as she put more wood in the stove to hurry the dinner. "An' he's fine lookin' too."

Anna nodded, though she had paid little attention to how the young man looked.

"Broad brow—heard that means good intellect," Mrs. Trent said sagely. "Fine honest eyes, no shiftiness in them, look directly at you. And a strong chin. Heard that a weak chin means a weak man. Nose straight and not too big. Good thatch of hair—but he keeps it nicely under control. Fine-lookin' man. Don't know when I've seen finer."

Anna drew her mind momentarily from the new book in her bedroom. She supposed he was a fine-looking young man. She hadn't given it much thought.

"Suppose every mother in the district will be settin' her cap for him," her mother went on, and Anna raised her head and gave her full attention to the conversation. Why in the world would the district mothers be setting their caps for the young man?

"They'll all be foistin' their daughters on him," her mother continued, "tryin' to get his attention with dinners and suppers and social invitations."

That's silly, thought Anna.

"You just watch," went on Mrs. Trent. "I'll just be willing to guess that come next Sunday, every marriageable girl in the congregation will have a new Sunday dress or bonnet—maybe both. You just mark my word."

"That's silly," said Anna aloud.

"Yes," sighed Mrs. Trent, "it might be at that." Anna did not notice the sideways look she cast at her young daughter. It was quite clear that they would not be in the running. Anna seemed to have no interest whatever in the young man—apart from the books he was willing to share.

Anna also didn't notice the look of disappointment or the sigh of utter relief as Mrs. Trent turned back to the stove. Anna couldn't read her mother's thoughts. *We won't need to be worrying about losing Anna. At least not yet. Not for a long time yet. It's a relief. I don't know how I would ever get along without Anna. And yet—* She sighed again.

❧   ❧   ❧

Mrs. Trent had been right about the neighborhood mothers and daughters. Anna had never seen so many new bonnets and new frocks turn up as she did the second Sunday the young interim pastor preached. Some girls had even discarded their simple braids and had their hair pinned up in becoming fashion. Anna looked at her lifelong friends and blinked in unbelief, but they only smiled coyly as though quite unaware of what they were doing or why they were doing it.

It didn't matter to Anna, but she wondered how the young man felt about all the flurry of excitement and silliness.

After the morning service—which included another fine sermon, this time on the young man Joseph—Anna waited, books in hand. She had finished both of them, reading the one to as many of the family members as wished to listen. The second one she had pored over after she had retired to her own bedroom at night. It was a wonderful book about Bible times and people, and she had learned so much about the culture of the day.

Now she was waiting for an exchange. But she could not interrupt the conversations of other parishioners.

"You may wait until you get your book," her mother had told her. "We'll go on ahead, and I'll get dinner on the stove."

Anna waited—impatiently, for every moment of delay cut into her afternoon reading time.

Finally the last family took departure, and the young man turned from the steps of the little church and moved toward the front of the small sanctuary. He did not see Anna waiting until she cleared her throat.

"Anna. I didn't realize you wished to speak with me," he said quickly.

"Not speak," faltered Anna. "I . . . I just need to . . . to exchange these books—with your permission, please."

He eyed the books she held out to him.

"You didn't like it?" he asked, indicating the second volume, the thicker of the two he had given her.

"Oh, I did—very much. I would have read it over and over again—if I'd had the time. But I would like to get on to the others and—and—"

"You did read it?"

Anna nodded.

"All of it?" His eyebrow raised in surprise.

She nodded again.

For a moment he seemed to question if the young girl was telling the truth, but her eyes returned his gaze, honest and open.

"You are a remarkable youngster," he said with admiration and then continued. "Did you understand it?"

"I . . . I think I did. At least most of it. I . . . I wasn't sure when I came to the part about . . . about the Incarnation. About the way they explained it. I mean, I know Mary was Jesus' mother, and God, by His Spirit, was His father, but I couldn't understand some of the words they used. I mean—well— I guess I find it hard to understand—but—but easy to believe."

He smiled. One of his full, approving smiles. "That is faith," he said to her. "Sometimes it is much easier to just believe without trying too hard to understand—at least all at once. God's ways are so far above man's ways that we can't always understand them with our finite minds. We need to just accept things as He gives them to us."

Anna nodded. She was sure he was right—but she wasn't sure just what he was saying, either.

"So you want a new book?" he was asking.

"If—if I could please," she answered.

"Come," he invited. "You can pick your own."

Anna would have liked to linger over the choosing, but she knew her mother was by now needing her help with the Sunday dinner. She let her gaze slide over the titles and settled quickly on a new book.

"Do you read this to the family?" he asked in surprise.

She shook her head. "I—I don't think the little ones would—would understand some of these words," she admitted.

He smiled softly. "I don't think they would either," he agreed. "Why don't you pick another of those from the top shelf. Maybe this one. *Stories of Jesus' Ministry*. Might they like that?"

"Oh, I'm sure they would," breathed Anna as she reached for the book. She had almost, in her eagerness for knowledge, chosen selfishly. Now she would have a book to study and a book to read to the rest of the family.

She thanked the young man profusely and turned to go.

"Anna," he called after her as she was about to leave. "What can you tell me about the Sturgeon family? I'm invited there for dinner."

Anna turned to him. "They live on the Main Road . . . about—"

"I know where they live," he explained gently. "Tell me about *them*."

Anna didn't know what to say. She moistened her lips and thought for a minute. What did he wish to know?

"They—they have four girls—" she began, but before she could even go on he was nodding his head.

"I thought as much," he said wryly and suddenly she thought he looked weary. Perhaps he had been spending too many hours over the stack of books on his kitchen table, concentrating too hard on his Sunday sermon preparation.

Chapter Four

A Brief Summer

Anna spent the summer listening to soul-stirring sermons and drawing deeply from the well of knowledge in the books she regularly selected from the young interim pastor's library. He knew as he shook hands with his parishioners that when he turned from the last one, she would be quietly waiting for him. Always he had a question or two about the last books she had borrowed, and she often amazed him with her perceptive comments and hunger for knowledge.

"What does it mean to be sanctified?" she asked him one Sunday. And another Sunday, "What is your position on predestination?" And still on another, "Do you believe that Christ will return pre-tribulation, mid-tribulation or post-tribulation?"

He scarcely knew how to answer some of her candid questions, but he was always honest and straightforward. If he was in the position of still sorting through some issue for himself, he told her so. Then he invited her comments on her studying. Anna was hesitant to share her opinions, and he had to draw her out. There was so much she didn't know. She was thankful for books that could give her enlightenment, even though the authors often disagreed between them on interpretations. Still, they did give insight.

But Anna was panicky that she would never make it through the big stack of books before the summer ended. Soon the interim pastor would be leaving for the city, wherever it was, where his seminary was situated, taking his supply of books with him. She hated to let them go. But of course she would welcome back the elderly pastor and his wife. Maybe she would even be able to discuss with them some of the things she had learned over the summer months.

More than ever, Anna wished she had been born a boy. If she had, she was quite sure she would have chosen to be a preacher. That way she could just go on studying and studying throughout her entire life. He had said that—and had told her on more than one occasion—a pastor must never, ever consider that he knows all there is to know.

"The more we study and want to learn, the more God reveals about himself," he had told her. "That is how we grow and mature in our Christian walk. One must walk in the light of God's Word, but how can we do that unless we know what the Word says and understand its meaning?"

He had written down verses of scripture that she was to look up in her own Bible when she reached home. She had found the verses. In fact, she had committed to memory some of them because she had considered the portions to be of such importance—and she would recite the verses softly to herself as she picked up a new book to study.

"Study to show thyself approved unto God" was one of her favorites. She was more than willing to agree with the scriptural admonition, throwing herself into the study books with heart and mind.

Anna was completely unaware of the glances that were cast her way as she waited for the young minister each Sunday. Girls older and prettier than she wished there were some way they could get equal attention. But neither Anna nor the young seminary student took notice. Their interest lay only in the knowledge that they both sought and shared.

꙾ ꙾ ꙾

"This will be my last Sunday," he said hesitantly. "I will miss our conversations. You have forced me to dig deeper than I have ever dug before."

Anna looked up with surprise showing in her eyes. She didn't understand the comment.

"You've asked some tough questions," he explained. "I had to really study to find some satisfactory answers."

"I—I didn't know," she began. "I'm sorry."

He laughed then, a soft chuckle of amusement. "Oh, don't be sorry," he hastened to say. "It was good for me. I sort of feel like—well, like I've got a head start on the year of studies. This has been a great summer for me. I feel—well, blessed that I was asked to take over Reverend Angus's work for the summer."

Anna wished she could ask him when he would be leaving, but she felt that it would be improper.

"When will the Anguses be back?" she asked instead.

"Wednesday. Then I will leave the next morning. I start classes a week from tomorrow."

Anna nodded. She had her answer. He and his books would soon be leaving. She dared not exchange the two she held for new ones. She wouldn't have time to finish them and return them.

"Thank you. Thank you so much for sharing your books over the summer," she said softly, holding out the two she held.

"You are more than welcome," he assured her. "Just wait till I tell the fellows at seminary that a young girl kept me on my toes all summer. They won't believe me."

Anna smiled shyly. She wasn't sure if his words were a compliment or merely teasing.

"I will miss you, Anna," he said simply. "I'm sure that I'd get more out of my seminary classes if I had you at my elbow, urging me on."

Anna found herself blushing. She knew she had no place in his seminary classes, and even the idea of being there made her embarrassed.

But he changed the topic quickly and surprised her by saying, "Would you like me to send you a new book now and then?"

"Oh . . . I couldn't—" she stammered.

"I could mail one now and then—or send it out to you with the Anguses when they come to the city. They come in every now and then for a convention or meeting. Take one now and send it back with them sometime."

"Oh, but I—"

"Go ahead," he encouraged. "The Anguses will be glad to act as courier. Send it back with them whenever you are through with it, and I will send you something else."

"If—if it wouldn't be too much trouble," Anna breathed, hardly able to believe the possibility.

"No trouble at all. I'll be glad to," he promised.

Anna chose a book as quickly as she could make her decision, then turned to him, unable to express her deep gratitude.

He held his hand out to her. "Goodbye, Anna," he said simply. "I'll be in touch."

Anna went home, a book tucked beneath her arm. The summer hadn't ended her study after all. She had a new book to read—and he promised that he would send another as soon as she was done with this one. Anna felt blessed indeed. The more she learned, the more she wanted to learn.

☙   ☙   ☙

A busy fall and winter kept Anna busy with canning and taking in the garden, cooking for the harvest crew, and long days of tucking things in for winter. Evenings often found her with old mittens and socks to be darned or new ones to be knitted. Then her mother spent a few weeks in bed. The doctor called it pleurisy. Anna worried, but carried on the double burden of looking after the household.

She did not have as much time to spend reading as she had wished. The winter days were much shorter now, and even the long evenings seemed to get taken up with necessary activities.

But when she could, Anna returned to her books. True to his word, Austin Barker sent new books periodically. And with the books came brief letters telling of his seminary studies. Occasionally the letters asked questions of Anna. What did she think of such and such a chapter? What position did she feel one should take on a certain issue? What was her understanding of a certain text? Anna always answered as best she could, but she felt so inadequate even to be discussing such important topics with a seminary student.

Anna always returned the previously borrowed book immediately upon receipt of a new one. She didn't wish to take advantage of his generosity.

Spring came. Anna heard the call of killdeers, the song of the robin. It would soon be time to plant the garden again. She loved the spring. Even loved the hard toil that it brought with it. It seemed to invigorate her—give her a new purpose in life. But she knew instinctively that it would mean less time in the books. Her mother needed her for the many household and garden tasks that awaited them.

Anna wondered that she had been humored for as long as she had. No other girl her age was given time to spend reading and studying. She felt deep indebtedness to her mother—and thankfulness to her father that he hadn't interfered with the arrangement. She determined that she would not presume on her parents. She would allow herself one hour of study—at night—after the usual duties had been accomplished. And she would work doubly hard at the many tasks that needed to be cared for.

Anna did indeed work hard in the kitchen, the garden, and at the scrub board in the yard under the spreading Manitoba maple. Some nights she was much too tired to spend even one hour in reading. But she tried to make up for it on other evenings.

The boys were growing. Adam, having completed his eighth grade, was finished at the local school. He was now doing a man's work at the side of his father.

Horace, the next in line, had taken over Adam's chores, and each boy shifted up the line, taking on added responsibility. Even young Petey, now three, had been given some simple tasks to perform.

And Mrs. Trent leaned increasingly on Anna. Both as co-laborer and as companion. She talked while they worked together, her mind skipping from one topic to another. Anna's active mind, often busy with her own thoughts, tried to concentrate so she might follow the conversation.

"That young minister isn't coming back this summer. Mrs. Angus told me. I guess that means Nettie won't get another chance at him. Mrs. Angus is slower than ever on that poor leg. Guess she won't get time off this summer though. Expect she doesn't have a granddaughter getting married this year. Too bad. The poor soul looks like she could use another rest. She works too hard. I told Mrs. Shehan that it isn't right for the church to expect so much of her. We should have a younger pastor's wife. 'Course that would mean a younger pastor. Wonder what his plans are when he finishes his seminary."

Anna soon realized that her mother had gone full circle.

"You know his plans?" Mrs. Trent asked Anna abruptly.

Anna shook her head.

"He doesn't mention them in his letters."

"No," said Anna.

"What does he write?"

"He tells about his studies. We—discuss the books. The teachings. What we think about certain ideas," explained Anna truthfully.

Mrs. Trent seemed to dismiss the comment as either too deep to be understood or too boring to consider.

"This is his last year?"

Anna agreed that it was.

"Then he must plan on taking a pastorate next spring."

"I would expect so," said Anna, then continued. "He hasn't said."

"Wonder if he'd consider coming back here," pondered Mrs. Trent. "He was a good preacher. Suppose he'll be lookin' for a big city church. Or they'll be lookin' for him. Even boys listened. Didn't squirm nearly as much. Poor Pastor Angus. He is a dear, dear man of God—but he loses his train of thought every now and then."

Anna's thoughts returned to her mother's earlier statement. It was true—some of her brothers had sat and listened to Austin Barker.

"Well, it would be worth looking into," continued Mrs. Trent. "One never knows unless one tries. Why don't you just sorta ask him what his plans are in one of your letters?"

But Anna could never feel free to probe into the plans of the young minister. If he wished to share his thoughts regarding his future, he'd do so in his own time, she reasoned.

❧   ❧   ❧

The second spring since Anna finished school drew near. Life continued on in the same way that it had, full of work that changed only with the season.

Anna still delivered the milk to the parsonage, taking full advantage of those enjoyable visits with the elderly parson and his wife.

And then one day she was surprised and confused by a turn in their conversation.

"We are going to the graduation ceremonies," Mrs. Angus told her. "Mr. Barker has asked if it would be possible for us to take you with us."

"Me?" exclaimed Anna incredulously.

"He said that you have a real interest in learning and might find it interesting to see a graduation ceremony. Would you like to go?"

"Well, I—I—I'll have to ask Papa and Mama!" exclaimed Anna.

She was excited and scared at the same time. It would be wonderful to see a real graduation ceremony. It would be wonderful to visit a seminary— even for a few hours. It would be wonderful to see another small part of the great big world. But she wouldn't fit. She really had no business going. She didn't know how to conduct herself in such circumstances. She didn't know what to say or how to say it. What to do. What to wear. Why, she likely didn't have one thing in her closet that would be fitting.

"I . . . I don't suppose—" she began.

"Mr. Barker will be writing a letter to your father and mother asking for their permission," the kind woman continued.

Oh no, thought Anna. *Mama would be just likely to say yes. She—she thinks that—that I—that I would just jump at the chance. But—* Anna looked down at her faded cotton. She hadn't done much growing over the last few years, but her dress was definitely too short—and too tight. Whatever would she wear?

But Mrs. Angus was speaking again.

"Last time I was down to visit my daughter, she gave me a couple of boxes of clothes that had been her girls'. Said if I knew of anyone who could make use of them—" The woman stopped and smiled at Anna. "If it doesn't bother you to wear hand-me-downs, we could go through the box and see what we might find."

Anna nodded, her throat tight. It wouldn't bother her at all to wear hand-me-downs. She guessed that she had never had a perfectly new dress in all of her life. Her mother had always sewn her things from garments passed on from one aunt or another.

She swallowed with difficulty and nodded her head.

"I'd like to go—if Pa and Mama say yes—and if you are sure that I won't be a bother to you and the pastor . . . and if we can find something in the boxes to fit," she admitted, but fear was still mixed with the excitement in her eyes.

Chapter Five

Preparations

Over the days that followed, Anna's emotions ran the gamut. From excitement and joy, she was plunged to doubt and despair. Then she would be swung back into the arms of exhilaration again, only to be dropped back to utter desperation.

The boxes of hand-me-downs proved to supply many nice pieces of material. Anna was much smaller than the two granddaughters of Mrs. Angus. But Anna had been taught to be a skilled seamstress, and with the help of her mother and Mrs. Angus, a fitting, though simple, wardrobe was designed and sewn. Anna was thankful and elated about that part of her dilemma.

But when thoughts of meeting so many strangers—so many educated people—assailed Anna, she floundered. If only she knew the proper rules for such occasions. She felt so inadequate, so backwoods, and she was too shy to discuss her lack of social skills with the kind Mrs. Angus.

At times she broke into a cold sweat just thinking about the upcoming events, and then she would determine to find some reason that she couldn't go.

Then her thoughts would swing back to the graduation service. It would be so exciting to be a part of it—even a small part—and she would be so proud of Pastor Austin Barker when he marched up for his diploma. Would it be something like her certificate? she wondered, and then blushed in embarrassment for even thinking such a thought. His would be much more grand and important.

No, she decided, she couldn't miss it. She just couldn't. She'd have to keep her eyes and ears open and notice what others were doing. Perhaps she wouldn't make any dreadfully big blunders. She would hang back and try to be as invisible as possible. She did not wish to embarrass the Anguses or her friend Austin Barker. He had been so kind to lend her his books and tutor her by letter.

Anna could tell that her mother was ecstatic about the invitation. She seemed to treat it like a coming-out, a debut for her only daughter. When Mrs. Trent talked about Anna's trip, her mother did not appear to be filled with Anna's many doubts. She sounded confident that her daughter would make quite an impression on the learned city people she would meet. She considered Anna to be dainty, attractive, gentle and considerate. What more could anyone want in a young woman? Anna knew by her mother's comments that Mrs. Trent's only regret was that she wouldn't be there to witness the entire three-day trip. So her mother made the most of the preparations. She bubbled and gushed with enthusiasm as she stitched dainty seams, adding lace where Anna felt no lace was needed, placing tucks where Anna felt they could do without them, pressing until beads of sweat stood on her brow when Anna felt that the garment was already smoothly pressed.

"You need new shoes!" Mrs. Trent exclaimed one day as she labored over the invisible mending of a lace handkerchief.

"But, Mama—"

"I saw a pair in town last trip I made. Just right to go with the dresses."

"But, Mama—"

"I've got egg money in the jar. Count it out. See if it's enough for new shoes."

"But, Mama—"

Mrs. Trent lifted her eyes from her needle for the first time. "Go ahead," she said, nodding firmly toward the corner cupboard. "No daughter of mine is going to shame the family by having worn-out shoes on her feet."

Anna laid aside the hem she was stitching in a newly sewn skirt and rose to do as bidden.

I wonder what she was saving the egg money for? she thought to herself as she moved to the cupboard.

There wasn't quite enough money in the jar.

"Well, we can spare a few of those hens," Mrs Trent said. "I was thinking of selling a dozen or so anyway. Take too much feed to get them all through the winter."

It's spring, Anna wanted to say, but she held her tongue.

"Tell Pa we need to make a trip to town. And tell him that we need to put a crate on the wagon for some of those hens."

But as Anna moved toward the door, her mother changed her mind. "Never mind," she said, "I need a stretch. I'll tell him myself. You go get yourself changed and ready to go."

She started toward the kitchen door and then turned to speak again, "An' while you're at it, get a pair of those fancy stockin's."

Reluctantly Anna moved toward her little bedroom. She felt terribly guilty that so much time, attention, and family money were being spent on her. She was so undeserving. What would she do with all the fancy new clothes after the trip to the city? Folks in the area wouldn't be expecting her to be so dressed up—not even for Sunday church. It did not occur to Anna that she would be dressed no differently than the neighborhood girls her age.

She changed her clothes, loosed her braids, and pinned the long tresses up in soft swirls. Mrs. Angus had shown her how to pin her hair, and her mama had her practicing. It made her look a mite older—more her real age—than the braids. But it also made her face look even smaller, and her blue eyes seemed to dominate her face. The only thing it didn't do was to make her long, straight nose diminish in size. Anna wished with all her heart that it would have.

Before leaving her room she reached for a book. If she was making the long trip into town, she might as well take full advantage of the time. She could even read to her father. He liked to discuss her new-found Bible knowledge almost as much as she did.

❧   ❧   ❧

It was late afternoon by the time they returned from town. Anna's new shoes were tucked safely in her lap. She had not released them all the way home, even though she and her father had enjoyed a vigorous discussion about Armageddon.

Her mother was in the yard. Anna wondered if it was coincidence or if the older woman could not wait to see the purchase.

"Did you get them?" Anna was asked as soon as the wagon had stopped rolling.

Anna lifted up her little parcel and nodded her head in agreement, her eyes taking on a shine.

The shine in Mrs. Trent's eyes matched Anna's. "Bring 'em in," she said with a nod of her head.

Brothers began to come from this direction and that, and they all seemed to have the same question. "Did you get 'em? Did you get 'em, Anna?"

Then the shout changed to, "Put 'em on! Put 'em on, Anna. Let's see 'em!"

"Go ahead," said Mrs. Trent, nodding her head toward Anna's bedroom door. "Put them on—with the stockings—and try them with that gray-blue suit and the frilly blouse that you'll be wearing to the graduation. Go ahead."

Anna went to her room, excitement making her heart pound. She slipped out of her clothes and lifted the lovely white blouse with its generous lacy collar and cuffs from its peg. She had never expected to own such a garment. She could scarcely believe it was hers even now. She slipped into it and carefully did each button. Then she let the beautiful gray-blue skirt slide over her head and settle into place at her waist. Her fingers fumbled with the hooks in her nervousness. She eased into the jacket, adjusting the lapels as she studied her flushed face in the mirror.

Carefully she eased on the new stockings. She

did not want to cause them damage.

The shoes came next. Anna looked forlornly at her discarded old ones. They were badly worn. Then she placed a tiny foot into the shiny new leather. It seemed to gleam up at her and she held her breath. She added its mate to her other foot and stood to her full height. Taking a deep breath she moved toward the door that separated her room from the kitchen.

A joyous shout went up from the assembled little crowd when she made her appearance. They were all there. Her mama—with Karl pressed tightly up against her skirts. Her papa—with young Petey held in his arms. Adam. Horace. Will and Alfred. They were all there—eyes turned to her door, watching for the moment of her appearance. Exclaiming their approval. Clapping their hands to share her joy.

Anna's eyes filled with tears. She looked around the room at the mended overalls, the brown bare feet, the faded apron over an equally faded dress, and her heart constricted with emotion. She wanted to run to her bedroom and throw herself face down on her bed. It wasn't fair. It just wasn't fair that she should have so much—and they so little. But there they all were. Cheering her on. Rejoicing in her blessings. Beaming because of her new wardrobe. What a wonderful family she had! To weep now would be to let them all down.

Anna forced a smile and whirled her way around the circle, presenting one dainty foot and then the other.

"Wow!" hollered Adam.

"You look like a princess, Anna," called young Karl.

Will and Horace clapped their hands and whistled, and Anna's mama did not even scold them for doing the forbidden—whistling in the house.

Even young Petey began to squirm in his papa's arms. "Want down. Want down," he insisted, and when his father lowered him to the floor he ran to Anna, crouched down, and reached out a pudgy childish hand to feel the shiny new leather, then looked up at Anna and grinned.

Anna noticed the toes protruding from Petey's worn shoes. He was the only one of her brothers who wasn't barefoot. "His feet are still too tender," her mama would say, and so Petey would wear shoes for at least the first part of the summer. But the shoes were Sunday hand-me-downs, and by the time they had reached Petey there wasn't much wear left in them. Seeing them now made a lump come again in Anna's throat, and she wondered how much longer she could hold back her emotions.

At last they let her go, each one returning to a task that had to be finished before the supper hour. Anna went back to her room and carefully removed all her finery. She felt like Cinderella after the ball—returning to her rags and her hearth of cinders. Her throat ached with the desire to cry. She cast a glance toward the fine things. The shoes were so stylish—so shiny. And the blouse and suit were—were almost like new. No one would ever know they had been sewn from someone's hand-me-downs.

But Anna could not shake off her feelings of guilt. She wished deep in her heart that she didn't have the fine things. They were a reminder of what the rest of her family did not have. If only everyone wasn't so—so kind—so benevolent. It wasn't so hard to slip into her rightful place in the world when she was dressed in her mended, faded cotton frocks. But when she was dressed in the fine clothes, the new shoes, the frilly blouse, she was confused. She felt that she was deceiving the world. That she was pretending to be something she was not. Anna could not help but wonder if the Lord, who knew who she really was, would disapprove of her sham.

For a brief moment she gave in once more to her feelings. *I'll not go,* she said to herself. *I'll just not go.*

But just as quickly, Anna could picture the hurt in her mama's eyes.

Well, I'll go, she amended. *But I'll just wear my own clothes.*

What had Mama said? Something about not allowing her daughter to bring the family shame. But wasn't it just as shameful to pretend to be something you were not? Didn't God judge the heart rather than the outward appearance?

And then Anna's eyes lit up. She could wear the clothes—for her mama's sake, just as long as her heart was right.

But, oh, it would be so hard to keep her heart right when—when folks were seeing her as one of them. When they were thinking she thought she was an equal. When they judged her by her outward appearance. When she would need to come back to her work cottons.

In spite of her strong resolve, Anna had to brush away tears before she could return to the kitchen.

The three traveled by train. Anna had never had such a wonderful experience. She had looked forward to the hours of train ride, thinking she would have all that precious time to read and read. But her eyes kept straying from the pages of her book. There was so much to see. She feasted upon the sights, the sounds, the feel of new freedom.

The Anguses seemed to be content to just sit back on the blue plush seats and relax from all their busyness. That was fine with Anna. She needed full concentration to absorb all that was going on around her.

The trip ended far too soon for Anna. Before she knew it the Anguses were gathering up their carry-on items and preparing to depart the train.

"We are to be met by friends—the Willoughbys. We will stay with them tonight," said Mrs. Angus.

Anna had already been informed of this, but she nodded politely. Mrs. Angus often repeated herself—but then she was getting forgetful.

"Mr. Barker was so sorry that our train was to arrive right when he was busy with graduation rehearsal," Mrs. Angus went on. Anna had heard that too.

Anna let her mind turn to the rehearsal. What did they rehearse? What needed practicing? Wasn't there just one way you could graduate?

"Ah—there are the Willoughbys waiting on the platform."

With the words from Mrs. Angus, Anna's heart began to pound. Now it would all begin. The strangeness, the confusion, the introduction into a world that she did not know nor hope to ever understand.

⚜   ⚜   ⚜

Anna got through the first evening in fitting form. No one knew of her inner agony. No one sensed that she felt overwhelmed by her new surroundings.

She had promised herself to keep her eyes and ears attuned to the manners and words of those around her and to follow their lead. What she did in actuality was to naturally keep her mind and heart open to the needs of others. Anna was never conscious of doing so. It had come from years of unselfish living, of practice within the home in which she had been raised, of an inner commitment to her God and His created people. It was as natural to her as her breathing. And so without thinking, she sought small ways to help, to reach out a hand of assistance, to give a tiny word of encouragement. To gently ease someone's burden. To naturally be polite and courteous.

And so the Willoughbys saw exactly what the Anguses had seen for many years. A slight yet not fragile person—well mannered and well groomed, looking out at the world with a pair of wide, honest blue eyes that accented a small oval face. A polite, gentle young woman with a kind, sensitive spirit, devoted to her God and considerate of others.

Chapter Six

Graduation

"The graduation service will be at ten," said Mrs. Angus. "That will be followed by a reception for the special guests of the graduates. Reverend Angus and I will be attending because of his part in the reception. You will be the guest of Pastor Barker."

Anna knew all that, but she smiled and nodded her head. Then an awful thought struck her.

"Does that mean I won't be sitting with you?" she queried.

"Oh, we can sit together for the service. At the reception we may need to sit at a separate table. I don't know the seating arrangements, but by then you will be with the Barker family, so you won't be deserted."

Near panic seized Anna. *The Barker family*. She had only thought of Mr. Austin Barker. She was sure she could feel reasonably comfortable with him. But his family? How many Barkers were there? Would she be among a whole group of strangers?

"Only his father and mother were able to come," went on Mrs. Angus. "He has three married sisters and a married brother. Austin is the youngest family member. Two of the girls are missionaries and the brother is a seminary professor."

If the words had been meant to encourage Anna, they had quite the opposite effect. How would she ever manage with such saintly people? Surely his father and mother must be—be extraordinary to have raised such an educated and devout family. Anna would not fit in at all. For one moment she considered taking to her room. But her mama would be so disappointed. She would expect a full description of the event when Anna returned home. No, Anna couldn't back out now. She steeled herself for what lay ahead and followed Mrs. Angus into the crowded sanctuary.

It was a long and glorious service. Anna loved every minute of it. She intently drank in every movement, her ears cocked to every sound. She must be able to give a full account when she returned home. But even with her intensity, Anna knew that she would never be able to do justice to what she was witnessing.

At last they began to award the degrees, names in alphabetical order. There were only three young men who preceded Austin.

"Austin Tyler Barker, by the authority that is invested in me . . ." the robed man was saying, and Anna felt her heart swell with pride as she watched the young man reach out to accept the hard-earned degree. And then the gentleman in the robe added a few more words that puzzled Anna, "Magna cum laude," he said.

Anna repeated the words over and over to herself. She wanted to be sure to remember them so that she could ask Mr. Barker. She did hope they weren't any kind of embarrassment to the recipient. Perhaps she shouldn't ask—maybe simply find some way to look them up for herself. The man on the platform hadn't used the words when speaking to the other three young men who had received their diplomas.

Anna heard similar words—at least part of them—again as they continued through the graduation ceremonies. On two other occasions the gentleman in his robes said "Cum laude" as he handed a degree to another young man.

Anna could hardly stand the suspense. She longed to lean over to Mrs. Angus and ask her about the strange words. But Anna had been taught not to whisper in church, so she held herself determinedly in check.

It was Mrs. Angus herself who broke the silence. "Cum laude means with honor," she whispered in Anna's ear.

Anna's eyes widened. With honor? That was very nice.

Then a new thought struck her. If "cum laude" was with honor, what was "magna cum laude"? She did hope it did not mean *without honor*. Oh, poor Mr. Barker if it should mean that. To have it announced right out in public for everyone to hear. What a shame! What an embarrassment!

At last they were standing, watching the robed and hooded young men make their way down the long aisles of the auditorium. She could bear it no longer. She leaned toward Mrs. Angus and whispered as softly as she could, "What does '*magna* cum laude' mean?"

The older woman could not hear her words and

Anna had to repeat them louder, her face flushing with embarrassment.

"What does '*magna* cum laude' mean?"

"That means with great honor," returned the lady, and Anna felt her heart leap. Her Mr. Barker was the only one in the entire graduating class to receive the greatest of honors.

※　　※　　※

Anna's emotions pulled her this way and then that way. She was anxious to meet Austin Barker again. It had been two years since she had seen him—even though they had faithfully exchanged letters in the intervening time. Yet she was nervous about seeing him again. She had totally forgotten he was so nice looking—that is, if she had ever really noticed before. She had been far more interested in his books than she'd been in him. But as he had stood on the platform, receiving the reward for his work of four years, he had no book in his hand. Anna was forced to see the young man himself.

Also, they were now in a different setting. One in which he was quite at home—but Anna was not. She was bound to be awkward and clumsy. She fervently hoped that she wouldn't embarrass him in front of his wonderful parents.

Again Anna wished she could just fade from the picture, but the crowd before and behind seemed to be moving them down the aisle and out the doors. Soon, ready or not, she would be facing the Barker family. Anna felt faint with anxiety.

Mrs. Angus was pressing Anna's gloved fingers. "We'll see that you get together with the Barkers before we leave you," she said in Anna's ear. "Mr. Barker will take over from there."

With a crush of people all around them, Anna thought they might not make it out alive. She had never been in such a crowd before. She felt as if she could hardly breathe and longed to escape the press and get out into some fresh air.

Anna wondered how the elderly woman was doing with her cane in the mass of human bodies, but Mrs. Angus seemed to be functioning all right. Anna reached out a hand to clasp the woman's elbow and give her a bit of additional support.

Reverend Angus was steering them both toward a side door.

"I told Pastor Barker we'd meet him over here," Anna heard the man say to his wife.

They made it to the indicated door and there was Pastor Austin Barker. He shook hands heartily with Reverend Angus, then Mrs. Angus, lightly brushing aside their hearty congratulations on his achievements. Then his eyes turned to Anna. She saw the surprise that he could not mask. "Anna?" he said, almost in disbelief.

Anna felt her heart sink. She had disappointed—or embarrassed—him somehow, and their time together hadn't even started. She wished she could leave. That the floor would just swallow her up. She forced her head to lift so that she could meet his eyes.

But it wasn't disappointment or embarrassment that she saw there. Confusion. Surprise. Amusement. Anna thought she saw all three reflected in his eyes in quick succession. And then he smiled.

"You've changed," he said simply.

Anna felt the color wash over her face. He knew that she had no business being dressed up in shiny new shoes and a lace-trimmed blouse. He knew she was pretending to be something that she was not. Maybe he *was* embarrassed—ashamed of her.

She met his eyes openly, honestly, trying to get him to understand that it was for the sake of her family that she had come as she had. She would go back to being "Anna" just as soon as she returned to her own farm home.

But Mrs. Angus was speaking. "Our little Anna has grown up," she was saying, but there was pride and satisfaction in her voice.

"Yes," admitted Pastor Barker, but Anna thought his voice still was not totally controlled.

"We must run. Our ride is waiting," said Reverend Angus, and Anna felt her heart quake.

I could go with them if you wish, she longed to say to the young man before her. *Or I could walk back to the Willoughbys. I'm sure I'd find my way.*

But she couldn't say the words. Anyway, he was still looking at her strangely; then he took her arm. "Come," he said. "My folks are waiting."

There was really nothing to do but let herself be steered through the milling crowd and out the door.

They did not speak again until Anna was presented to the senior Barkers.

Mrs. Barker looked from her son to the young woman and back again; then she smiled and stepped forward.

"Anna," she said, extending her hand. "It is so nice to meet you. We have heard so much about you." And she shook Anna's hand warmly, one hand resting gently on Anna's shoulder.

Then her eyes lifted to her son and she spoke again. "We had come to think of you as a child, my dear. We thought of you as our little Anna for such a long time, and now I see that we should really address you as Miss Trent."

Austin Barker shuffled slightly. "Well—two years does make a difference," he mumbled.

Anna stood in confusion. She wasn't sure what was happening.

"Would you prefer to be addressed as Miss?" Austin's mother was asking.

Anna managed a wobbly smile. She didn't understand the significance of the statement. She was Anna. Why would Pastor Barker's mother want to change that?

"Anna is fine," she finally volunteered.

The hand on her shoulder extended to slip around her, and Anna felt herself given a warm hug.

"Good," said Mrs. Barker. "Anna it will be. We have our little Anna still."

She seemed pleased with the thought, and Austin turned Anna to meet his father.

❧   ❧   ❧

Later Anna was presented to many of Austin's fellow classmates. She was aware of eyebrows lifting. Of teasing smiles and playful nudges. But Anna was unable to understand the responses.

Are they laughing at me? she asked herself. But she found them all to be so kind, so courteous, that she couldn't believe it to be so.

No. It had something to do with Austin. For

some reason his friends were teasing him. Anna puzzled over it but at last was able to push it aside. She couldn't sort it out. She didn't understand the customs of this new world that she had entered.

❧   ❧   ❧

"May I see you back to the Willoughbys?" Pastor Barker was asking her.

It had been a long confusing day and Anna felt more tired than if she had done a huge laundry over the wooden washboard. And her feet ached in the shiny new shoes.

She managed to nod her head and prayed silently that they wouldn't have to walk.

"I've borrowed a team," Pastor Barker was saying. "If you don't mind, I thought we could take a bit of a drive. This is the only opportunity I'll have to see you, and I did want to have a chance to—to discuss—to—to talk—a bit."

Anna nodded again. She was so thankful to hear that they would be comfortably riding.

They were out of the busy town and into the calmness of the countryside before Austin spoke again. He seemed to hesitate a bit—as though not knowing where to start, but then just blurted out, "I—you—I suppose you noticed my surprise when I saw you today."

Anna nodded.

"Well—like my mother—I have thought of you as—well as a—a little girl—a child. I—I guess I described you to them in that fashion."

Anna's eyes widened.

"Well—I see that—that I've been—been badly

mistaken. You are far from a child, Anna."

Anna did not know what to say. She was sorry that she had let him down.

"I'm sure—with your perception—you also noticed the surprise and amusement of my fellow classmates."

"I did," Anna managed to say.

"Yes—well—you see—the joke was rather on me. I had spent two years telling them about—about this—this brilliant, eager young student that I was coaching—and then she turns up—an attractive young woman. No wonder they wished to razz me a bit. They could see for themselves that writing to you, teaching you, was no sacrifice. I suppose they now doubt my good intentions. Was it your beauty—or your brain? Any one of them would have been glad to be your teacher."

Anna swung her head around to look directly into Austin's face. Was he serious? He appeared to be.

Anna felt total confusion.

"Well, I want you to know," Austin continued in subdued tones, "that I still admire your keenness, your searching, your aptitude for spiritual things. You have taught me much, Anna. You have helped me to grow and stretch—almost as much as the theology texts. I want to thank you—and if—if you have no objections—I would like to continue our correspondence in the future—even though—even though you have—have grown up."

Anna reached down a gloved hand to smooth her fine gray-blue skirt. She dropped her eyes to her lap and answered shakily, "Of course."

She sensed Austin shifting beside her, but she did not look up again.

"I—I still don't know where I'll be going. We are to be given assignments this week. There are at least three churches open."

Anna's eyes widened. There had been nearly thirty young men who had crossed the platform to receive their degrees. What would happen to all of them if only three churches were available?

"What will the others do?" she asked before she could stop herself.

"What others?" asked Austin.

"The ones who won't get a church. Don't all of those who graduated hope to be pastors?"

"Oh—yes. But fellows come from many denominations to attend this seminary. They will go back to their own churches. Their own denominations. They will be pastors all across the country. Actually, we have only five young men from our church. And Reverend Angus wishes to retire—if a replacement can be found."

Anna felt a pang in her heart at that news. She had learned to love the Anguses. Yet she knew that they needed a rest—deserved a rest. She sighed. She would miss them.

"Most of the churches want a married man," Austin went on and Anna nodded. She knew that her home church would find it hard to welcome a bachelor into the manse.

"There are only two of us who aren't married. I think we'll be asked to start mission works somewhere. Our district feels the need to reach new communities. It will be quite a challenge. Even for the new works they would like to—to send couples.

They hope to start five new churches over the next ten years. That's a rather ambitious goal. But the need is great."

Anna had never heard him talk so much. She looked at him and nodded, encouraging him to go on.

"I think that I'd enjoy starting a new work," he continued, then quickly added, "but I have left it in the hands of the Lord . . . and the church leaders. I am willing to go wherever they wish to place me."

Anna thought of the "magna cum laude." Surely they would place him in some big city church where his intellect and abilities could be used to full potential.

Darkness was beginning to settle in around them. He seemed to sense it at the same moment she did.

"I must get you back," he said quickly. "They will think I have kidnapped you."

Anna smiled to herself. *A preacher—kidnapping?* It was a strange and amusing thought.

"You are taking the train home tomorrow?"

"In the morning," answered Anna and then held her tongue until he had turned the team and they were once again on the road home.

"Maybe I will be able to read tomorrow," ventured Anna. "I had told myself that I would have all those wonderful, empty hours to fill with reading on the trip here, but I couldn't. I just kept—kept being distracted by all the—the strangeness and all the fascinating things around me."

Her voice had risen as she spoke, excitement making it tremble.

"Like?" he prompted.

"This woman boarded with this huge bundle," said Anna, her gloved hands indicating the size. "It looked like laundry—or something—but we hadn't gone far when it started to wriggle. Then the strangest noises, low and—and kind of guttural—started to come from it. She fussed and hushed and tried to push it under the seat, but it refused to budge—and then out came a head. It was a turkey gobbler. A full-sized gobbler. She had smuggled it on to the train."

Austin threw back his head and laughed.

"Did she get away with it?" he asked her.

"They made her get off at the next stop," said Anna, sadness tempering her voice. "I felt sorry for her. What could one little old turkey hurt, anyway?"

From there on they talked of Anna's train ride, then switched to the book she had brought to read, and soon their discussion had turned to the rite and merits of baptism by immersion.

Chapter Seven

Changes

Something had changed! Anna had expected to come back home to things as they had always been, but the familiar rut now seemed uncomfortable. She didn't seem to fit anymore.

Her family wanted a full account of all she had been witness to, and Anna was able to accurately and vividly describe the sights and the sounds of her adventures, but she was unable to share the change that had taken place within her. She didn't understand it herself.

Outwardly, she was the same Anna, back to simple garments, swinging a hoe or lifting laundry from boiling lye water in a steamy kitchen. She was still an obedient daughter, quick to respond when her mother gave an order or her father voiced a request. She was there when her little brother stubbed his toe on a rock, or one of the older ones needed a hand with forking the hay up into the loft. But a part of her, a very small part of her, was somewhere else, reliving another world. A world that she could not dismiss now that she knew it actually existed.

But it wasn't "her" world. It was the world of Reverend and Mrs. Angus. The world of the Willoughbys. The world of Austin Barker and the other young men who soon would be taking up the challenge of the ministry. Anna felt a sadness steal through her whenever she thought of this new world.

She had not been home for long when she received a letter from Pastor Barker. He had been given his assignment. Excitement spilled out from the words on the page. He would be starting one of those new churches in a small town called Carlhaven. Anna left her room and entered the kitchen to ask her father where Carlhaven was and learned that it was a little town, roughly forty miles away, but forty miles to Anna seemed like a very long way.

"Used to be called Carl's Haven when my pa was a boy," went on her father. "Fellow by the name of Carl Pearson settled there. Liked the spot, I guess, to give it such a name. Name got changed some over the years. When the town finally put up its little sign over the railroad station, they forgot the *s* and just made it one word."

Anna was glad for the bit of information. She wondered if Pastor Barker knew that piece of local history. She decided that she would pass it on to him in her next letter. She went back to her room to finish reading.

"I am to start right away," he enthused. "I can hardly wait to see if 'the preaching of the Gospel' works as well in practice as it does in theory."

Forty miles. He would be forty miles away preaching the Gospel. Anna began to pray for him and his new church every night.

❧   ❧   ❧

The Anguses did retire. A new pastor and his wife were sent to their little community. It was the first pastorate for Reverend and Mrs. John Clouse. They brought with them enthusiasm and plans for growth, and Anna enjoyed her trips with the milk deliveries in spite of the fact that she missed the Anguses.

She had just returned home from one of those deliveries when Mr. Trent came in the door from a trip to town and handed Anna a letter. She had just received a letter from Austin Barker and couldn't imagine two coming so close together, so she looked at the handwriting and realized at once that it was not from him. But in the corner of the envelope was an unknown address, and there above it was the name, plain as day, "Barker."

Anna frowned as she tore open the envelope. Was someone trying to play a strange trick on her? She certainly knew Pastor Barker's handwriting after all the years of correspondence.

But the letter was signed simply, Austin's mother. Anna's frown deepened. She did hope nothing had happened to Austin.

It was so nice to meet you after hearing about you for so many months. I must say that I was a bit surprised, as our son had described you as a young girl—but as he said, two years does make a big difference. I must admit that I was rather pleased to find you a young lady. And a kind and gracious one at that. We do want to keep in touch.

As you can imagine, mothers are rather protective of their offspring, especially the baby of the family, and Austin is my "baby." Yet I thank

God that He has called him into the ministry. I know there will be many difficult things for him in the future, but I can honestly say that I trust God to lead him as He wills.

I am sorry that so many miles separate us. It would have been so much nicer for my husband and me if God had called Austin to serve nearby instead of almost a thousand miles away. He's not awfully good about letter writing, either. Perhaps it is unfair of me to ask, but it would mean so much to me if you could drop us a line now and then and sort of pass on to us what is going on in his life—as well as your own, of course.

We were so delighted to meet you. We have thought of you as our Anna for many months and hope that we may always do so. May God bless and lead you in all your future plans.

Lovingly,
Austin's mother

Anna's frown deepened. It was such a strange letter. Why was Mrs. Barker asking her to keep in touch? And why was she assuming that Anna would be able to pass on information about her son?

It was true that they were still writing, but Anna was sure that soon his new ministry would be taking more and more of his time, until writing letters to a young girl who was interested in theology would be laid aside.

It all was very puzzling.

But, Anna mentally added the senior Barkers to her list of people, like Pastor and Mrs. Angus, to whom she wrote.

⚜   ⚜   ⚜

Unexpectedly to Anna, over the months that followed, Austin's letters came more often rather than less frequently. Anna waited for every one, as it told of the young pastor's ministry in the new town. She prayed earnestly for the names that appeared on the paper. She felt anguish as the building they had hoped to purchase went up in flames and another place had to be sought. She grieved when an elderly parishioner, Austin's prayer warrior, passed away.

In a strange way, Austin's ministry was also her own. She shared the joys, the disappointments. She sensed the triumphs and the struggles. She prayed as she had never prayed before, even though forty miles separated them.

"I would like to see you," Austin wrote in one letter, causing Anna's heart to race. "I hope to borrow a team to come over. The train would take forever as we are on two different lines. I'd have to go on into Cabot and then on out again. It would be time-consuming and costly. So I thought that I would try to drive over. Is any time better than another? I really would like to make it as soon as possible."

Anna answered quickly and assured the young minister that he would be welcomed at any time. That same week he arrived. Anna was unprepared and was embarrassed that he found her feeding the hens in her faded cotton.

But he didn't seem to notice. He smiled and held out his hands to her.

"How are you?" he asked and she smiled shyly in response.

"You look more like the little girl I remember,"

he teased, tugging gently on one of her braids.

She nodded. Her fine garments were hanging on wall pegs, a worn-out cotton sheet secured about them to keep off the dust.

"I must look a mess," Anna managed.

"Not at all," he said softly. "I—I think that you look—quite—"

But Anna did not want to hear his assessment. She quickly turned toward the house and interrupted his statement.

"Come to the house. I'll put on the coffee. Mama has just finished taking fresh bread from the oven. I remember how you used to enjoy it when I'd bring a loaf to the parsonage with the milk."

He turned to follow her.

"Do you still deliver milk?" he asked as they moved toward the kitchen together.

"Oh yes. If I have the time. I enjoy the stroll. But sometimes one of the boys takes it."

"Do you have a delivery to make tonight?"

She looked at him. What was he asking?

"Yes," she answered truthfully. "I had planned to go right after the supper hour. But I can stay here and send my brother—"

"Oh no. I'd like you to go. I mean—if you don't mind, I'd like to go along with you."

"Of course," responded Anna, remembering that he knew the new pastor and his wife. It was only reasonable that he would want the chance to chat with them. Maybe that was his reason for this visit.

They reached the kitchen and Pastor Barker was welcomed by Anna's mother.

"So good to see you again!" she exclaimed, shaking his hand heartily. "How are things going in that new church? We've been remembering you every day in our prayer time."

Austin thanked her sincerely and began to give her snatches of news about his new community, his church, and his parishioners.

Anna moved about the kitchen, preparing the coffee and the fresh bread and jam. But she listened intently as she worked. It was good to have a first-hand report.

✣   ✣   ✣

"I think I'll go out to the field and walk in with your father," Austin said as the supper hour drew near.

Anna nodded. She supposed that it was terribly boring for a man to hang around the kitchen while supper was being prepared.

"He's in the west field," she responded, and the young man picked up his hat and left the room.

"He's a fine young man," observed her mother as soon as Austin had left them. Anna nodded. He was a fine young man. But he needed a wife. Needed a good wife to help him in his ministry. It was not easy for a man to work alone. Anna had been praying privately that God would provide the right young woman for Pastor Barker. Someone to work as a helpmate. Someone to help carry his load.

At the same time that Anna prayed, she knew that a woman coming into Austin's life would mean that she would be gently pushed out. She would miss him—dreadfully. But it was a small price to pay for furthering the effectiveness of his ministry.

Anna would ache for a while—but she would still pray.

❧   ❧   ❧

He was the one who lifted the two pails of milk as they started their journey toward the town manse. Anna's hands felt strangely empty. She didn't know what to do with them, so she tucked them in her apron pockets. She had meant to lay her apron aside, but she had forgotten. At least it was her newest apron, worn over a rather attractive blue gingham. She had changed before supper and had loosened her braids and pinned her hair up, too. She did look less of a child, she'd decided, but her eyes still looked too big for her face and her nose was too long.

If Austin thought so, he made no comment. He'd only smiled when he saw her working about the supper table when he'd come in with her pa.

"Do you still miss the Anguses?" he asked her as they walked together.

"Yes," she answered truthfully. "It's not that I don't like the new minister. I guess . . . I guess I was just so used to—" She broke off her thoughts and then continued. "Do you know that the Anguses had been here ever since I was a little girl? To me they are . . . they are the living example of what—what a minister . . . and his wife should be."

He nodded in understanding.

"And now this new couple," he said with understanding, "it's like . . . like a new marriage. You have to work out a totally new relationship."

Anna laughed. "Well, it is a new relationship,"

she admitted. "Having never been married, I can't speak for that marriage part."

"I'd like to change that."

Anna's head came up from the dust that lifted around her feet. She looked at him directly. Evenly. What was he saying?

He stopped and set down the pails. Then he reached out his hands to her.

"Oh, Anna," he said and his voice sounded husky. "I have been thinking and praying until— until— But it all makes so much sense. No one understands me like you do. No one feels the heartbeat of my ministry. I know that you are young. But—but God keeps reminding me that you are also—also perfect."

"Oh, Pastor Barker," said Anna quickly, her face going pale. "I am not perfect." Her mind began to sort through a long list of shortcomings.

But he reached for her hand and drew her nearer. "For me, and for what God has called me to, you are," he insisted.

But Anna shook her head. "No," she argued. "I'm not—not perfect for—for anything."

"Then we will be wonderfully teamed," he laughed softly. "I'm not perfect either."

But Anna was in no mood to share his teasing. Her head was still spinning from the shock of his question. What was he thinking? Asking?

"I—I have already asked your father," he said, seriousness returning to his face and voice.

"You—you asked my pa?" exclaimed Anna incredulously.

"I did. That's why I went to the field to meet him."

Anna felt a shock wave go all through her being. She couldn't even speak to ask how her father had responded.

"He gave us his blessing," went on Austin, reaching for her other hand. "Now, all I need, all I am hoping to hear . . . is your yes. Will you marry me, Anna? Will you share in my ministry—my life?"

Anna was stunned. She had prayed for a wife for Pastor Austin Barker. She had never dreamed that *she* might be that wife. Had never dreamed that he would ever want her. She was needed at home—to help her mama. Anna had never thought of her life in any other context. But her father had given his blessing. Did that mean that she was released to go? Did it mean that God might have other plans for her? She didn't know what to say. How to answer.

A feeling of total inadequacy overwhelmed her. She thought of the good Mrs. Angus. She, Anna, could never measure up. She could never be what a pastor's wife must be. She was little and scrawny and plain. She had no talents or abilities. No. No, it was out of the question. How dare she even consider it for a moment?

"I—I can't," she faltered. "I—I—"

"Please, Anna," Austin was pleading. "Please. I have come all this way for your answer. I love you, Anna. I guess I have for much longer than I care to admit—but I didn't realize at first that my 'honor student' had also stolen my heart."

"What would your mama and papa say?" managed Anna.

"My mother will be thrilled. I think that she understood how things really were—even before I did." He tipped his head and smiled again. "I even think she might have been doing a lot of praying of late. And my father—he was impressed with you as well. They will both be very pleased—if you say yes."

It was totally unthinkable. Austin would be so disappointed when he learned of all of her inadequacies.

"I—I don't know how to be a pastor's wife," Anna stumbled.

"And I don't yet know how to be a pastor," replied Austin with a bit of a chuckle as he gently eased her closer. "We'll learn together."

"But you don't understand," quickly cut in Anna, pulling back. "I—I don't think I can learn. I—" She stopped and shook her head, her eyes turned to his with pleading for understanding.

"I love you, Anna," he repeated. "And I have prayed—much—and if I understand the will of God, He has seemed to indicate that I could at least ask you."

Anna shook her head in bewilderment. She looked at the man before her, her eyes wide, and tried to swallow. He looked so serious. He had been praying. Anna's world was still spinning around—but she looked up at Austin, evenly, candidly, and nodded her head, her blue eyes looking intently into his. She swallowed, fighting back her fear. She felt dreadfully unworthy, but if he wanted her to share his ministry—if God truly approved of her being Austin's wife—then she would not hesitate any longer. She would do the best she could do—for the God who loved her—for the man she—yes, she loved.

Chapter Eight

Beginning to Serve

They were married in Anna's church. Reverend Angus came back to perform the ceremony and Austin's parents came the long thousand miles to share in the joy of their youngest son.

"We are so pleased that you are now really 'our' Anna," Mrs. Barker exclaimed, holding Anna in a warm embrace. Anna felt delightfully welcomed and a good deal nervous. Would she ever be able to live up to their expectations? She, a simple country girl? She would try. She would try with all her heart, but she still was worried that she would fall far short of what a minister's wife should be.

The new Mr. and Mrs. Austin Barker left soon after the wedding. Anna could not believe that she was really saying goodbye. That she would not be there to tuck Petey into bed that night or to deliver the milk to the pastor's family. To flip the pancakes for the morning breakfast or take the feed to the hens. Who would take over her many tasks? It would be too heavy a load for her mother to carry alone. Anna felt confused. She wanted to share in

Austin's life and his ministry. Felt that she was doing the right thing in becoming his wife. But what of her overworked mother? Who would be there to help her? Searing guilt nagged cruelly with each thought of leaving her mother.

They traveled the forty miles by horse and buggy, staying a night in a small hotel in a little town on the way. Austin apologized for the simple accommodation, but Anna didn't understand why. It was her first experience in a hotel and the room seemed quite adequate to her. It was also the first meal she had ever eaten in a hotel dining room. She couldn't believe that she would be given the choice of an entire menu and found herself unable to decide.

"You pick for me," she whispered to her new husband. "All these different choices are confusing."

He laughed and decided on the roast beef for both of them. They even had apple pie for dessert. Anna left the table feeling overfed. She refused to waste food by leaving any on her plate.

The next day they were up early and on their way to the new parsonage. Austin apologized about it too. "It is a very simple little place," he warned. "Only three small rooms. Very small rooms. A kitchen—where the stove takes up half of the space, a living room—that has to serve as parlor, family living, and my library all in one, and a bedroom without the benefit of a closet."

It sounded fine to Anna. She was sure that she'd find some way to make it "homey." She thought of Mrs. Angus and her African violets and wished there was some way for her to get a few slips to start growing them in their own little home.

When they reached the parsonage, Anna saw
that Austin was right. The rooms were small. So
small that Anna wondered where she would find
room to unpack her few belongings.

She removed her new bonnet, another gift from
her mama's egg money, and changed from her traveling suit. She carefully hung the clothes that had
served her at Austin's graduation on the few hooks
on the wall, spreading the worn sheet about them
to keep the dust off. Then dressed in a nearly new
cotton print, she set about her duties as the wife of
the community minister. In her mind's eye was the
good Mrs. Angus—her model and mentor. Anna
knew deep within herself that she would never
measure up, but she determined to try her hardest.

๙ฦ   ๙ฦ   ๙ฦ

The small congregation was meeting in the local
schoolhouse. Austin introduced her to the group on
their first Sunday.

"I have the pleasure of presenting to you my
lovely bride, Mrs. Anna Barker," he said to them
and invited Anna to stand and turn to greet them.

Anna felt the color wash over her face as she
slowly rose and faced them from her front-row seat.
There they were. Austin's people. Her people. She
smiled at them shyly and was gratified to see their
warm response.

She sat back down in her seat and tried to com-
pose herself before she had to meet them individ-
ually at the door.

A glimpse toward her husband filled her heart
with pride. He was such a fine-looking man, such a

good man. Anna could hardly believe even yet that she was actually his wife.

And then her thoughts traveled on, making her squirm slightly in the pew. *They will all be wondering what he ever saw in me. And I'm sure I wouldn't be able to explain it. It's a mystery to me, as well.*

❧   ❧   ❧

They settled into their new life, their new roles as husband and wife. Anna found little ways to make the most of her small home and Austin felt more comfortable as pastor. When it came time to go calling, they hitched their mare to the new one-horse buggy and set out together. As far as Anna could remember, Mrs. Angus had always called along with her husband.

Friday came—the day that Austin set aside each week as the final day of sermon preparation. He had to spread his Bible and books all over the kitchen table, and Anna didn't know how she would manage to bake her batch of bread.

I must change my baking day, she said to herself. *Instead of Tuesdays and Fridays, it must be Mondays and Thursdays. But how can I ever bake bread and do the laundry all on the same day?* Anna and her mother had always washed clothes on Mondays. She gave the matter some thought.

I guess there is nothing sacred about washing on Monday, she decided at last. *From now on I will wash on Tuesday.*

But it did seem odd to Anna. If her washing did not appear on the clothesline bright and clean early on Monday mornings, would the town folks think she was negligent in her household tasks?

When Anna had wrestled a bit further with the problem, she finally concluded that Austin's sermon was more important than her washday. She switched the laundry to Tuesday.

Wednesdays would be set aside for visiting their parishioners. Saturdays for cleaning and making preparations for Sunday. Thus their week was generally established. They soon discovered that there were constant adjustments to the schedule as various needs arose from families in the community.

But it was the evenings that were the bright spot of Anna's day. After the daily tasks were completed, the lamps lit, Austin spent time studying from his shelf of books. Anna, of course, was free to help herself to any of them—and she often did. On those occasions when her hands were busy with mending or sewing, Austin read to her. Lively discussion followed as they exchanged ideas with enthusiasm. They often found that those conversations ended with one or the other—sometimes both—taking a little different point of view than they had when they had begun.

"You're good for me, Anna," Austin often told her. "You force me to think."

Anna could only shake her head. Austin was the thinker of the family.

But Austin continued to encourage Anna to study and to set aside a good portion of her time "mining for gold" among his many books. In fact, more than encouraging, he depended upon her. Every new concept that he discovered, he shared with Anna. Back and forth, pro and con, each candidly and openly expressed their views until they felt they had reached a reasonable and biblical conclusion.

And Austin always wanted Anna's response to his Sunday sermons, both before and after they were delivered. She read them carefully, critically, not with an intent of tearing them apart, but to judge if they progressed easily, were insightful, yet able to be clearly understood by the least educated member of the congregation.

"You know my thoughts and intent," Austin said to her. "You know as well as I do what I am trying to say. Tell me. Am I saying it?"

Anna felt strangely honored to be assigned such a task. She also felt dreadfully unworthy.

⚜   ⚜   ⚜

The new congregation continued to meet together in the schoolhouse, but Anna knew Austin longed for the day when they would have their own little church building.

"It will be difficult for us to really feel we are a real congregation—members of the Body—until we have our own gathering place," he often told Anna, and Anna nodded, willing to accept his assessment.

He repeated this statement one evening as Anna sat mending worn socks by the light of the kerosene lamp. Austin had been studying at the kitchen table nearby but rose to his feet, pacing back and forth from the window to the chair where Anna sat. She knew he was agitated, but she waited until he was ready to express his feelings. Her needle continued to ply in and out of the wool stocking.

"We need a church," he said at last as he ran his

hand through his heavy dark hair and let his fingers rest on the back of his neck.

Anna waited a moment, then said quietly, "We *have* a church, Austin."

He looked at her a moment, then smiled a bit sheepishly as she went on, "But our church does need a place of its own to meet."

Austin nodded, then said, "But we are so few, with so little. We'll never manage it."

"Remember the loaves and fishes," Anna commented, tipping her head slightly.

Austin chuckled. "The loaves and fishes. I wasn't planning to feed them, Anna. Just provide them with a place to worship."

"That's feeding," Anna said seriously, not backing down. "Remember what Christ said to Peter, 'Feed my sheep.' What you intend is spiritual feeding—and that is even more important than the physical feeding."

Austin's chuckle died away and his face too became serious.

"You're good for me—you know that?" he said with feeling, and he bent and kissed Anna on the top of her head.

Anna continued to mend.

Austin took up his pacing again, his brow furrowed in deep thought.

"So how do we get our hands on these loaves and fishes?" he said, wheeling to face her.

In the short while that they had been married, Anna had come to realize that it was difficult for Austin to be patient. She sensed the agitation in him now—and she admired it because she knew the reason for it. She knew his eagerness to be fruitful

in his ministry. She knew how difficult it was to
wait for something that he felt was so important to
his people. She fervently wished that she had a
ready solution. But she continued to sew, calmly, se-
renely, as she pondered carefully his question.

At last she raised her eyes. "In the case of the
loaves and fishes—they were brought to Him," she
said evenly.

"Are you saying—?"

"In other instances, people were told to 'go and
do.' "

"So?" said Austin, giving his shoulders an impatient shrug. "Are we to 'go and do' or sit idly by
and—?"

"We don't know that yet, do we?" said Anna plac-
idly.

"So we just—?"

"Pray," filled in Anna. "Pray for direction and
ask our little congregation to pray with us."

For a moment Austin's frown deepened. He began to pace again.

Anna laid aside a finished sock and reached for
another one.

"You think we should share this with the people?" he wondered.

Anna nodded.

"You think they will understand the necessity
for a church?"

"It *is* their church."

Austin paced a few more steps and swung to face
her. Slowly a smile began to spread across his face.
He ran his hand through his hair again and rubbed
at the back of his neck.

"I've been thinking it's mine, haven't I?"

"Have you?" said Anna, raising wide eyes to his.

"You know I have," he said, reaching out to touch her cheek, but there was lightness in his voice again.

"Actually, my statement was just as wrong," conceded Anna. "It really won't belong to the congregation either. This is *God's* church."

Austin nodded his head.

"So . . ." he said at last. "If He thinks that a building is needed, I guess He can come up with the loaves and fishes. Right?"

Anna smiled softly. "He might ask us to be involved—a little bit," she answered. "He did use the lad—and He did put His disciples to work."

Austin nodded again. The strain had left his face. He crossed the short distance that separated them and knelt by her side, reaching for the hand that held the woolen sock.

"This is going to be tough for me," he admitted. "I never was long on patience."

"Yes, I noticed," Anna teased and squeezed his hand.

Austin smiled and went on. "Promise me you will—will try to hold me in check. I need you, Anna. I need to—to borrow from your strength—your—your wisdom and patience."

Anna released her needle and thread and ran the fingers of her hand through his hair. She couldn't understand how strong and able Austin could be seeking to draw from her meager strength—but she knew she would be there for him to the best of her ability.

❦   ❦   ❦

Though she loved her new life as Austin's wife, Anna missed her family even more than she had prepared herself for. Her thoughts were continually going back to the farm kitchen where she knew her mother would be bent over a steaming ironing board or a hot kitchen stove. How was she managing to do all of the work alone? It had kept both of them busy from sun-up to sun-down—and even then they often got behind.

She hoped that the growing boys were giving some assistance, but she knew her pa counted on Adam and Horace to help him in the fields. And Will and Alfred were needed for all of the farm chores. That left only Karl and Petey. They were still too young to be given much responsibility.

At times Anna felt overwhelmed by guilt and concern. Had she done the right thing to leave her mother? Wasn't one to honor one's parents?

Yet both her father and mother had seemed to feel that she was doing right in accepting Austin's proposal—both had seemed proud to have their daughter join a man of the cloth.

Anna felt such confusion.

But even as she struggled to try to sort things out in her thinking, she knew if she had stayed at home, had said no to Austin, that she would have been devastated. Now she couldn't imagine life without him. She loved him with all of her being. She ached to sustain him, to support him, to be helpmate and companion. And yet she felt so inadequate.

Surely the people expected more from a minister's wife than she would ever be able to give. They were so kind—and so pleasant. But right now they had no church building, no organ, no room for Sunday school classes. When they did have their own place, had a *real* church service, then they would expect the minister's wife to take some leadership. Perhaps play the organ, teach classes, organize a woman's sewing circle.

Anna could not play a note. Had never had her hands on a keyboard. She had never taught Sunday school and had little confidence in her ability as a teacher. And she certainly had never been involved in a sewing circle except to sit in a corner with two or three other children and listen to the ladies talk of local prayer needs when her mama took her along. No, Anna was certainly not in a position to be of much help to Austin in his ministry—and the actuality of a *real* church building would serve only to draw it to everyone's attention.

Chapter Nine

Calling

The next Sunday after he had completed his sermon, Austin talked with the congregation about his desire to see them have their own place of worship.

"It doesn't need to be a fancy building," he told them, "but a place that is dedicated strictly to the worship of the Lord. A place where we can have Sunday school classes and Wednesday night prayer meetings. A place our children will view as God's house—not the schoolhouse. A place where someone can slip in during the stress of the week and kneel at the altar and talk things over with God. A place where we as God's people can meet with Him."

He paused and looked at his small flock.

"We need to pray for God's direction," Austin went on. For one quick moment he glanced toward Anna and their eyes met.

"We do not want to rush ahead of Him. Not that we could. We do not have the finances—the wherewithal—to do this task on our own. We must have the Lord's help.

"I'm asking you all to pray. Pray for guidance and direction—and you might ask for a miracle or two." Austin stopped to smile at his people. "It is going to take more than one miracle if this is to be accomplished."

Anna felt that his appeal was effective and she knew, because she knew the man, that it was sincere and came from his heart.

The people seemed hesitant to leave after the service. Anna heard excited murmurs on all sides. The idea had caught fire, but the cluster of people buzzing around her seemed to be no nearer a solution to the problem than she or Austin.

In spite of the excitement generated, they left the church with their problem unresolved.

Anna was thoughtful as she walked the boardwalk to their little home down the street. Austin had asked for a few minutes alone. Anna knew he wanted to get started in seeking God's direction.

☙   ☙   ☙

Dinner, stew again, was already simmering on the back of the stove, so Anna had little to do to get the meal ready. She wished she could serve fried chicken now and then—or a small piece of roast beef. Then she chided herself for her ingratitude. She should be thankful for the stew. The vegetables had come from the local store. There wasn't much for variety. And stew was as far as she could make their weekly offerings stretch. Yet they had never gone without.

Help me to be thankful, Father, she prayed in contrition.

But she couldn't help but wonder if Austin was as tired of stew and soup as she was.

If only I had a garden, she mourned. *I could*

raise my own vegetables. Then I could use the offer-
ings on something else . . . perhaps a bit of meat now
and then, or—

"Yoo-hoo!" A shout from across the street interrupted her thoughts.

Old Mrs. Paxton stood waving her cane to at-
tract Anna's attention. Mrs. Paxton did not attend
the church services in the schoolhouse. She was a
crotchety, sour woman with a sharp tongue and a
mean stick. She used both on local youngsters or
bothersome dogs whenever they came within reach.

Anna crossed the street, realizing that it was
much easier for her than for the elderly woman to
walk the rutted road.

"Hear you're planning on a new church." The
woman's words assailed Anna before she had even
reached the sidewalk.

Anna nodded, her smile fading slightly, wondering how the news had traveled so quickly.

"We are praying about it," she said evenly.

"Too uppity for the schoolhouse, I take it," the
woman accused.

Anna wished that she could have ignored the
call and had not bothered to cross the street.

"No, not too uppity at all," she answered as cour-
teously as she could. "We just feel it would be better
for the people—for the children—if we had our own
building so that we could—could have Sunday
school classes and—"

"Went to Sunday school when I was a child," the
woman hissed. "Never helped me any."

"I'm sorry," whispered Anna.

"Sorry? Sorry for what? That those Bible myths
told in Sunday school don't make a bit of sense?

That this—this farfetched tale of a God is all a hoax? He doesn't exist any more than—than the Blue Fairy does. All this church business is just a way to pad some man's pocket."

Anna's temper rose a bit as she thought of another dinner of vegetable stew. Pad a man's pocket indeed! But she smiled again.

"I'm sorry—" she began again, her eyes searching the face of the poor angry and bitter woman before her.

To her surprise, Anna's anger had changed to an attitude of love and pity. Her soft words only seemed to make the woman angrier.

Mrs. Paxton raised her cane and for one instance Anna found herself flinching and bracing for the blow.

The cane lowered again and the woman tapped the ground with all of her force.

"God took everything I had," she spat out. "Everything. My husband. My children. *Everything.*"

There was a moment of strained silence. Anna began again in a soft yet firm voice. "But that's impossible," she said.

"Impossible? I suppose you're going to tell me that your loving God would never let bad things happen. That—"

"No," said Anna, shaking her head. "No, I won't tell you that. But if He doesn't exist, how could He possibly do all of those horrid things?"

Wide blue eyes clashed with angry brown ones. Anna held her ground. She could see the intense anger that burned in the soul of the woman as her face flushed, her body trembled. The cane in her hand rose slightly, then fell back to the ground. Without another word to Anna, she turned and hobbled as quickly as she could toward her swinging gate. Anna did not watch her go. She closed her eyes tightly and bit her lip.

Oh, Father, she prayed earnestly, *did I say the wrong thing? I had wanted so to help her—but now—now I have made an enemy. Forgive me, Father. Show me what to do.*

Anna heard the gate shut with an angry bang. Then the cane rapped its way up the wooden walk.

Anna started back across the street with a heavy, guilty heart. Austin would soon be home for dinner. She had to dish up the stew and tell him about Mrs. Paxton.

🌿   🌿   🌿

The only thing that brought them a change of diet was the "calling." Every Wednesday for sure, and often on other days when there was a special need in a home, Austin hooked the mare to the buggy and they made a call. They were usually offered a meal, sometimes both dinner and supper at two different homes. At the least, they were served tea.

Anna welcomed those times, more for Austin's sake than her own. She almost envied the farm women who had fresh eggs and milk to cook with. What a difference it would make to their diet if she had access to farm products.

One day Austin came beaming into the kitchen.

"Guess what?" he said to Anna. "I met a new man in the store today. Mr. Parks introduced us.

Told the man I was the new preacher. At first he seemed a bit distant, but we talked about the weather and the crops and such things, and when he was about to leave he said, 'Say, Parson, I'm not really that interested in your church, but my wife sure likes to have lady company. Why don't you and your wife come on out for supper next week?' I nearly dropped over, right then and there."

"Oh, Austin," said Anna, reaching her hand out to grasp his arm. "That's wonderful."

To that point, their efforts to encourage more people to join their congregation had been without success. Anna knew how important the new contact was to Austin.

"We set the night for Thursday," went on Austin, his excitement showing in his eyes.

Baking day, thought practical Anna. *I will need to get up earlier to get the bread out of the way.*

They were both mildly anxious as the day approached. They so wanted to make this family feel accepted and interest them in spiritual things. Anna began her bread early that morning and had it baked by one o'clock. Then she washed and prepared herself for the journey. The Lawes lived a good way out of town, and it would take them more than an hour to make the drive.

Austin appeared in the kitchen doorway from the bedroom, his Sunday suit brushed and his tie carefully arranged.

"I was wondering," said Anna thoughtfully, standing before him in her best house dress, "if—this time—since he says he isn't interested in church—if we should go just—just as neighbors."

Austin's fingers paused in their fumbling with

the cuff links of his white shirt.

"What do you mean?" he asked. Before she could answer he hastened to add, "You'd better get changed. We need to be going."

"But that's what I mean," Anna said. "I *have* changed."

Austin looked at her, his gaze traveling up and down her cotton dress.

"I've decided that this once I'm going to try something different. Instead of entering a farm kitchen so dressed up in my Sunday clothes that I can't give a hand with the supper lest I get chicken fat on my dress, I'm going prepared to help."

Austin looked dubious but Anna held her ground. "And I was wondering if maybe you should wear one of your—your older suits—or even a pair of work pants so you could—could go with the man to the barn—maybe fork a bit of hay to the cows—or—or carry a bucket of water to the pigs."

Anna stopped and watched carefully for Austin's reaction. He looked at her as if he thought she had lost her mind.

"But a pastor is supposed to be . . . a little different from the rest of his people. Set an example. There's a standard that needs to be maintained. We represent the Lord. We were taught—"

"It was just a thought," said Anna with a shrug of her shoulders. "I can change quickly while you get the buggy."

But Austin stared at her for a moment, his face losing its doubtful expression. "It's worth a try," he said finally. "Nothing else has worked. We've called at almost every home in the community—and not one more person has been added to the church." He nodded and said again, "It's worth a try."

Austin made haste to change from his Sunday suit.

"Is this all right?" he asked as he rejoined Anna in the kitchen.

Anna looked at him and smiled at his flannel shirt and carefully mended work pants. He hardly even looked like a pastor.

Then doubts began to assail her. Maybe this was a serious mistake. She wrapped a loaf of the fresh bread in a snowy white dish towel, praying inwardly that she wouldn't spoil things for Austin. Oh, if only she were wiser about being a minister's wife.

᭟ᵛ᭟   ᭟ᵛ᭟   ᭟ᵛ᭟

In spite of Anna's second thoughts about her suggestion, the visit went well. Anna presented her loaf of fresh bread and moved easily into the kitchen to help with the supper preparations. Austin walked casually to the barn with the farmer, chatting comfortably about the livestock as they went. Anna, looking from the kitchen window, saw Austin slopping the pigs and forking hay. She smiled and prayed that God would give wisdom to both her and her husband.

Charles and Mandy Lawes had four young children. Anna made friends with them immediately. The three boys brought a longing to see her own brothers again and the little girl captured Anna's heart, chattering as though she had known her all her life.

The supper hour was friendly and sociable. The

children were well behaved at the table, and the adults were able to visit easily. When the meal finally ended and Anna had helped with the dishes, Austin announced that they must get started back to town. It was a long drive and they would be making part of it by moonlight.

No mention was made of the little congregation that desperately longed to reach out to those who did not attend church.

"Just a minute," said Mrs. Lawes as she scurried about her kitchen. "Have some of this fresh milk. And some eggs—Charles, get some eggs from the milk house."

Anna felt tears sting her eyes.

"The next time we're in town, we'll pick up the pail and bring you more," promised the woman, and Anna was afraid that the tears would spill over.

"Thank you so much," she murmured sincerely as she accepted the gifts.

"They are nice people, aren't they?" Anna commented as they drove toward the small town. She held the eggs in her lap, unwilling that even one should be cracked or broken.

"They are," nodded Austin.

"They've asked us back again," Anna went on.

"Do you think we did wrong in not talking about the Lord or the church?" asked Austin soberly.

"I don't know," said Anna quietly, shaking her head. Austin was the one who knew such things. "I—I think that if you should have spoken—God would have shown you. I—I mean—you didn't hold back because—because you were ashamed or—or uncaring or anything."

Anna hesitated.

"Every other call, we've made our position clear," went on Austin. "I would hate to think that I failed by not expressing my faith now."

"I think that it's important for them to feel—loved—accepted—as they are. As God gives us opportunity we will share our faith. We'll pray for that."

Austin nodded and clucked to the mare.

Chapter Ten

Reaching Out

Humming contentedly to herself, Anna lifted the sweet-smelling custard pudding from the oven. She couldn't wait to taste it. It had taken the last of her eggs and milk, but it would be worth it. It had been so long since she had been able to serve her husband a dessert. She could hardly wait to see the look on his face.

Her mouth responded to the delicious aroma. But she steeled her resolve to wait till she and Austin could taste it together and put the bowl in the kitchen window to cool.

Before she could turn from the window, she noticed Mrs. Paxton hobbling down the street, her cane thumping the board sidewalk and her face set in discontent.

"Poor soul," breathed Anna. "I have never seen such a living picture of misery."

Just as the thought raced through Anna's mind, she saw the woman stop and turn slightly. Her head lifted and Anna saw the wrinkled face wrinkle even farther as the woman sniffed the morning air. She stopped, turned farther, and sniffed again.

She smells my custard, thought Anna and reached to remove the dish from the window. It seemed cruel to torment the woman with the smell.

"I wish I had more eggs and milk," she said to herself. "I'd make her some."

As the custard cooled, Anna could not get the face of the old woman, her nose lifting to inhale deeply, from her mind. It was almost time for Austin to return for supper before Anna made up her mind. She lifted two dishes from the cupboard and filled one as full as she could. That would be for Austin. Then she spooned the remainder in the second dish, laid aside her apron, and started across the street.

Mrs. Paxton answered the knock, her usual scowl on her weathered face almost making Anna back away. But she held her ground, her smile determinedly in place.

"I—I made some custard for supper," Anna said simply. "I brought you some."

The expression on the face before her did not change—though Anna thought she might have glimpsed a brief light flash in the eyes and she definitely saw the nose twitch. Without a word the woman reached out, accepted the dish, and closed her door.

Anna turned and walked back through the dust of the street to her own kitchen. Though her mouth had been watering all day, Anna willed away all longing for the dessert. She really didn't need it. Stew would do just fine.

🌱   🌱   🌱

"It's an eyesore, that's what it is," Anna heard Mr. Parks say as she entered his store.

"A broken-down mess," agreed Mr. Werner.

"And right in the middle of town like that, too."

"Was a day it was a pretty good building," added an old gent Anna did not recognize.

"Be a choice location if it was worth anything."

"What is it?" asked another who was unknown to Anna.

"You mean what *was* it?" said Mr. Parks. "It was a store—and a good one. Now it's empty—or full of junk, I don't know which."

"I've thought it would be a good idea to put a notion in some prankster's head some Halloween to sorta put a match to the thing." That comment came from a younger man near the door.

Mr. Parks' head came up, a shocked look on his face. "You do that and you might burn the whole town," he cautioned.

Other heads turned, some of them spotting Anna hanging back hesitantly. "Mornin', Mrs. Barker. Help ya?" asked the storekeeper. Anna came forward.

"Just a few potatoes—and an onion," she replied, offering her coins.

There was complete silence until she had made her purchases and picked up the small bag. Just before she slipped out the door the conversation picked up again.

"Can't anything be done?" Anna heard someone ask.

"We've tried," said Mr. Parks with a sigh. "The whole town has tried. Ain't no reasoning with that woman. Can't even have a civil conversation with her. She refuses to sell and she refuses to spend a penny to fix it."

"Maybe she doesn't have the money," someone asked sensibly.

"Mrs. Paxton?" Mr. Parks snorted. "Money ain't what she's short of. He was a good businessman. Sort of a shyster, but a sharp businessman. When he died he left her rich. I mean *rich*."

Anna closed the door softly behind her. It was hard to believe that the shabby old woman across the street was rich.

Anna let her eyes rove over the building in question. It truly was an eyesore. About the worst-looking mess Anna had ever seen on a main street. The roof was beginning to sag, shingles were missing, the door would have swung on one hinge had it not been nailed in place with large spikes, the windows were broken and patched with chunks of rotting board. Even the walk up to the door that ran the few feet from the town boardwalk was rotting and broken. It was a sad mess. A disgrace to the town. Anna didn't wonder that other businessmen were concerned about it.

But her thoughts went back to the woman. In a way, the building was much like its owner. Worn. Defeated. Unloved and uncared for. Broken and seemingly discarded. Anna decided to drop her groceries off in her kitchen and then cross the street to pick up her custard dish.

❧   ❧   ❧

Anna had to rap twice before she heard the familiar thumping of the cane.

The woman shoved her face out the crack of the door without comment.

"I—I just came to see if—if you wished me to pick up my dish," said Anna, wondering if her bright tone sounded forced.

"Oh," the woman murmured, turning from the door and leaving it on its own. It must have been on a slant, for as soon as she released it, it swung farther open. Anna was able to see into the room.

She had not consciously formed the thought in her mind, but she realized that she had expected the inside of the woman's house to look much like her tumbledown main-street-vacated store. Instead, she was looking into a neat and tidy kitchen. The furniture was old but cared for, the table and cupboard cleared of all clutter. Dishes gleamed on the wall shelves, reflecting the afternoon sun. But most surprising to Anna was the off-street window. It was filled with blossoming violets.

"Oh, you have violets!" exclaimed Anna before she could think.

The old woman stopped mid-stride and turned to face her. "You like violets?" she growled.

"I—I—" Anna stumbled. Had she made another blunder? Then she contained her nervousness and went on with a smile. "Our pastor's wife always had violets. Beautiful ones. Whites and pinks and blues—every color. Ever so pretty. I always used to admire them. I—I've never had any myself, but I've always wished—well, that I had gotten some slips from her."

"Ain't so easy to do—slip violets," the old woman said as she turned and thumped her way toward the cupboard.

"Come in—and shut the door," she threw over her shoulder.

Trembling, Anna obeyed.

"Did yer pastor's wife have one like that one?" asked the old woman, pointing with her cane.

Anna followed the direction. Apart from the others, as though sitting on a throne among commoners, was the most beautifully formed violet Anna had ever seen. Its petals were creamy white, lined with a delicate purple fringe, frilly and full and perfectly formed. Anna breathed in slowly.

"No," she almost whispered, approaching cautiously. "No, she never had one like that."

The old woman had a difficult time hiding her smile.

"It's wonderful," breathed Anna. "Absolutely beautiful."

"I did it myself," said the woman. "Took years—but I kept crossing and mixing until I got that."

"You must be very proud," breathed Anna.

"Proud?" The old woman snorted. "No one left to be proud to. Ain't nobody who cares what an old woman does putterin' about in her kitchen."

Anna didn't know what to say in response, so she took what she hoped was a safe course. "Are you working on others?" she asked.

The woman nodded.

"I—I would love to see them," Anna said hesitantly.

"Haven't bloomed yet. You never know what you'll get until they bloom."

Anna nodded. "Well, when they do—would you—would you mind if I—if I see them?"

"You can see 'em if you like," the old lady responded. "Won't hurt them none to be looked at."

"Thank you," said Anna.

The old woman handed Anna her custard dish. Anna waited for some comment but none was forthcoming.

Anna walked toward the door and heard the cane thumping behind her. She saw a heavy chain hung listlessly on the doorframe. Anna assumed the woman would surely put it into place the minute the door closed behind her.

As she stepped outside, she turned with one more smile before the woman could push the door shut. "I do hope you enjoyed the custard," she said.

"I did," said Mrs. Paxton, and the door swung shut.

Anna smiled. It wasn't a "thank you" but it was enough.

꽃   꽃   꽃

"Those boys are making trouble again," said Austin as he put the mail on the kitchen table. Anna turned over the letters to see if there might be one from her mother. There was none. Both envelopes were addressed to her husband and looked official.

She lifted her eyes to Austin's, questioningly.

"They were tormenting poor old Mr. Fischel again. And when I arrived and scolded them a bit, they turned on me."

Anna's eyes darkened. She knew which boys her husband meant. They seemed to have time on their hands and were always hanging around the streets looking for some kind of trouble and making it if none was readily at hand.

She was sorry Austin had been placed in a position where he'd had to scold. But of course he couldn't stand by and watch the boys bother the nearly blind Mr. Fischel.

"What happened?" asked Anna in concern.

"Well, there they were on the south street, two of them crouched on each side of the walk, a rope between them, and the others were taunting and calling and telling Mr. Fischel that he had dropped something behind him. Of course, they were trying to get him to retrace his steps . . . and then trip over the rope."

"Oh no," breathed Anna. "He could be badly hurt. How could they be so cruel?"

"I don't think that cruelty comes with difficulty for that bunch," said Austin shortly.

"What did you do?" asked Anna.

"I told them they should be ashamed of themselves. Then I walked Mr. Fischel home."

Anna nodded.

"But they called after me, 'Goody, goody preacher. Thinks God is up there chalking up points.' I didn't make any comment and they finally tired of their game. But I feel bad. I had so hoped to help them, and now . . ."

Anna thought of the troublemakers. They had never bothered her as yet. But she had seen them teasing younger children and even town dogs and cats.

"Last week they had the Parks' cat up a tree throwing clods of dirt at her," said Anna.

"I don't know why their parents don't watch them more carefully," commented Austin.

"That's the trouble," said Anna. "Two of them are from the family at the edge of town. From what

I hear, their pa is far too busy to know what they are up to. And one is the Collins boy. He doesn't have a father. Another is a Fallis. He lives with his elderly grandmother. They are the regulars, I believe—and the worst of the pack. Other town boys, with nothing to do, get drawn in from time to time."

"Well, something should be done about them," insisted Austin. "Mr. Fischel could have been seriously injured."

Anna nodded. She knew it was true, but she also worried about the boys. Something certainly should be done—before they got themselves into serious trouble.

❧ ❧ ❧

The next morning when Anna started out for the store, she stopped in horror at a message scrawled on their front yard fence. "Hey, Preach," it said. "Drop dead."

Anna's breath caught in her throat. She wondered if Austin had seen the words. Embarrassment flushed her face. She felt as if she had been publicly disgraced, slapped, slandered.

Instead of proceeding to the store, she returned to her kitchen and got a pail of hot soapy water and an old brush. She scrubbed and scrubbed to remove the ugly words.

Oh, dear, she fretted. *What can we do? We'll never be able to help them if we make them our enemies.*

All day she prayed and thought. She did not wish to bother Austin while he was buried in his books, but when the supper hour came and they raised their heads from the table grace, she took a deep breath and began.

"What those boys need is something to do," she started. "Papa always said that it is idle hands that find trouble."

Austin cocked his head slightly, then smiled. "So you are going to put them to work hoeing town gardens?" he teased her.

"No," said Anna. "I had play in mind rather than work."

"Play?"

"They have nowhere to play," Anna informed him.

"So where can they play?"

"We have an empty lot behind us," said Anna.

"It's a weedy mess. No one could play there."

"Exactly!" agreed Anna. "It has to be cleaned up."

Austin had stopped eating to listen.

"So . . . you think they will clean it up?"

"No," said Anna. "We will."

"We will?"

"Why not?" asked Anna stubbornly, her eyes holding his.

"It belongs to the town," Austin reminded her.

"Then we need to ask the town for permission," said Anna. "Do you wish to put in a request—or do you want me to?"

"You're serious, aren't you?" said Austin curiously.

Anna only nodded.

Austin laid down his fork. "Then you'd better share your plan with me. Entirely. So I know what I'm asking for when I go to the town fathers."

Anna placed her fork beside her plate and reached to take her husband's hand. She leaned forward slightly, her eyes glowing with the excitement of her plan.

"Well, first we have to get permission to use the lot. Then we need a cleaning crew. At first it will be just you and me, but when others see that we are really serious about helping the town youngsters, then maybe they'll pitch in, too.

"We'll need a sign—right away—so that the children . . . the boys will know what we are doing. 'Carlhaven Sports Block, a Safe Place to Play, Dedicated to the Town Young,' or something like that." She paused a moment to organize her thoughts, then continued.

"We'll clean it up and put in a ball diamond. Maybe even get donations for a ball and bat—or a football—or whatever. At the far end we could even put in a swing or two for younger children—and a sandbox. We could do all sorts of things if we get enough people behind it. The more we can get involved in it the better our chances of making it a success. Folks will feel that it is *their* project and they'll pitch in and lend a hand. We might even have a fund-raiser . . . a picnic or pie social. We could set up a committee. We—"

"Whoa," said Austin, raising his free hand. "You are way ahead of me. I'm still back there somewhere on the cleanup."

Anna smiled and took a deep breath. "Oh, Austin. It could work. I'm sure it could. I mean, we . . . the town, has never done anything for the children. No wonder they are roaming the streets."

Austin picked up his fork and speared a potato

from his stew. "I'll talk to the town fathers," he promised. "It sure won't hurt to try."

The town officials were pleased that the young minister was serious about meeting the needs of the children in this practical way. Anna heard all about the meeting when Austin reported to her at the supper table.

"At first they seemed really hesitant—doubtful—but gradually they saw the advantage of the plan. I guess the mayor started things going our way. 'It's a good idea,' he said. 'And the lot is just standing empty. Might as well be put to use. It's an awful weed patch anyway. But it sure is going to take a lot of work.' "

"I told them I was willing to be the first volunteer.

" 'Put that in the minutes,' the mayor nodded to the town secretary.

"I thought he was just referring to my volunteering for the job, but then he went on, 'The lot is to be turned over to be used as a playground.' Then he turned back to me. 'Anything else, Pastor Barker?'

" 'A couple of things,' " I said. 'We'd like permission to put up a sign right away, announcing our plans for the area. And we'd appreciate the assistance of the town in raising funds to buy equipment.'

"That seemed to shake them up some. 'What sort of equipment?' The town banker seemed the most worried.

" 'A bat. Balls. Perhaps a swing or two. Maybe a sandbox for the younger children,' I told them, hoping that I had remembered all the things on your list.

"Heads began to nod.

" 'How do you propose we raise those funds?' asked the schoolteacher.

" 'Voluntary donations,' I said. 'Maybe a fundraiser of some sort. Perhaps we could set up a committee.'

"The silence didn't seem very promising to me, but then one head after another began to nod. The mayor even smiled.

" 'I like it,' he said. 'The lot is yours. Go ahead and get started. We'll see if anything comes of it.'

"Well, it wasn't exactly a strong endorsement or a commitment for backing, but at least it's a start. I thanked the town council and excused myself."

Anna's face beamed as she listened to the account. She was so pleased that they had official permission. She was very proud of Austin for handling the situation so well.

Chapter Eleven

Struggles

The very next morning, Austin was out in the vacant lot, his old trousers tucked into the tops of his boots, a worn work shirt rolled up at the sleeves. Anna was busy making the sign, anxious for the town to know what was going on in the weedy lot.

The unruly "gang" dropped by midmorning. "Hey, Preacher," the taunts began. "You lookin' fer your dinner?"

"You diggin' yerself worms?"

"Here, Preach," called one of them, tossing a rock in Austin's direction, "eat this."

They left when they found that all he did in response was to smile and wave his hand.

After finishing her sign, Anna hastened to take it to Austin along with his hammer, some nails, and a stake. The sign looked quite good, considering the material she had to work with.

But when they came to resume their toils the next morning, the stake had been pulled from the ground, the sign broken in three pieces and stomped on repeatedly, and all of the debris that Austin had carefully scythed and raked to a pile had been scattered again across the lot.

Anna could have cried.

Back to work they went—Anna with her small stock of paints and Austin with his scythe and rake. That evening they did not leave a pile of debris behind them. At the close of the day, Austin set a match to the waste and they stayed to watch until the fire had consumed the dried weeds and grass and was totally out. Then Austin pulled the stake with Anna's sign from the ground and carried it home.

Anna was so tired she had little energy left to prepare the supper.

"Tomorrow is Wednesday," Austin observed as he washed off the day's grime at the corner basin. "Should we put aside the calling this week and concentrate on the lot?"

Anna considered the idea for a few moments. "No," she said at last. "I don't think we should allow it to interfere with our visitation duties. We'll just have to fit it in when we have time."

Austin nodded. "I agree," he responded as he ran the rough towel over his hands and face. "So, where do we call tomorrow?"

"Mrs. Dobber hasn't been well. Perhaps we should check on her. Nettie asked me on Sunday if we could stop there if we get a chance."

Austin nodded. It seemed that their day was all arranged.

⚜   ⚜   ⚜

The thumping on the door didn't sound like a fist rapping, more like a stick banging. As Anna hurried toward it, the thought that it might be the neighborhood boys, up to some other unkind trick, crossed her mind.

But when she opened the door she was surprised to see Mrs. Paxton, raised cane in hand.

"One of them's ready," said the woman without preamble, and Anna had to quickly sort out the meaning of her words.

The violets!

"Oh," she smiled, reaching for a towel to dry her hands. "May I see it?"

But the elderly woman was already thumping her way down the walk on her return trip home.

Anna removed her apron, threw it on a kitchen chair, and followed her neighbor.

It was a pale blue flower, with a heavy fringe of white around the ruffled edge. Anna thought it was beautiful.

"Isn't quite what I had in mind," the old woman said gruffly.

"But it's beautiful," Anna remonstrated sincerely, wishing she could reach out and touch the delicate blossom but fearing that she would be reprimanded, perhaps rapped across the knuckles with the ever-present cane.

"Pretty enough," said the woman, and for the first time ever Anna thought she heard some softness in her voice.

"Do you name them—as you create them?" asked Anna.

The woman looked up, a startled expression on her face.

"What for?" she asked.

Anna shrugged. "I don't know. I just thought that—well—roses have names. And Mrs. Angus always knew the names of her violets. She'd introduce me to them—sort of. 'And this is Woodland Snowdrop and this is Pink Lace.' I don't know if they already had names or if she named them."

"They have names," responded Mrs. Paxton. "Least when you buy them, they have names. When you do your own . . ." She didn't finish.

"I think they should have names," Anna dared to continue. "It must be rather sad to be nameless."

"You talk like they were people," said Mrs. Paxton, looking at Anna rather suspiciously.

"Isn't that how you think of them?" responded Anna without turning her face from the flower. She was sure that it was, but would the woman dare to admit it? "Like friends? Or family?"

The old woman stirred restlessly but did not answer the question. "You can name it if it pleases you," she finally responded and Anna felt honored.

"Oh, could I? I would love to. If—if you're sure you don't mind."

"Doesn't mean I'll be calling it that," the older woman quickly retorted.

"Of course not," replied Anna softly. "But I will enjoy thinking of it—with a name. Let's see. It is so blue. Such a soft, yet bright blue—and with that lovely fringe. It looks like a lady in a shimmering crinoline."

Anna lifted her hands and folded them in front of her face as she thought deeply.

"What about Azure Princess?" she asked the older woman.

"Awful big name for such a tiny flower," the woman responded, but Anna noticed just a hint of humor in her tone and that she did not argue.

❧　　❧　　❧

The Barkers continued to call on the Lawes. At supper, the parson was even asked to say the table grace, and on more than one occasion, Austin had a chance to remind the couple that they would be more than welcomed to the town fellowship.

"We've been thinking about it" was the usual reply, but the Barkers never saw them in the church service.

However, the Lawes did continue to supply milk and eggs, and Anna was so thankful for the welcome addition to their daily diet. Whenever she had a bit of milk and a few eggs to spare, she made a custard, and always she took a generous dish of it across the street to Mrs. Paxton.

❧　　❧　　❧

Anna's visits with Mrs. Paxton became more frequent. She even wondered, at times, if she didn't see the older woman's eyes light up when she opened the door.

Their conversation usually was of violets. Anna longed to turn it to more personal issues and to things of God. She knew the woman still harbored deep bitterness over events of her past.

Anna did not feel free to ask about those events. She knew instinctively that thoughts of them still held much pain. But she did want to have the opportunity to present the truth of God's love to the sorrowful woman.

One day, Anna decided to try. She gave her best efforts, choosing her words carefully, but later as she reflected on the conversation she felt she had done a very poor job.

"Mrs. Paxton," she had said, "I've been praying a lot for you over the last several weeks. I—I feel great concern for—for—" Anna was interrupted.

"You needn't!" snapped the woman.

"But—but I do. By your own—admission you have—have pushed God out of your life. You have chosen to turn your back on Him. To . . . to deny Him."

"And that's my business," continued the woman, her eyes flashing darkly.

"But it's my business, too," insisted Anna, her throat constricting with emotion. "I—I have been— we have all been—commissioned to—to share the Gospel with those we—care about. And I care—I deeply care about you. I—"

The woman straightened her bent shoulders as much as she was able. She thumped her cane angrily on the floor.

"Look, Missie," she said, and she lifted the cane and shook it at Anna, "I don't mind our little visits. But you start prying and prodding into my personal affairs and I swear I'll lock the door next time I see you coming."

"I—I'm sorry," breathed Anna quietly, but she did not back away from the dark, piercing eyes. "I will not speak—if I am forbidden to speak—but I will continue to pray."

The shadowed eyes continued to glare at her, but the cane gradually lowered. Then the woman turned away.

"Pray all you want," she almost hissed. "He doesn't answer anyway."

"Oh, but He does . . . if we let Him." Anna could not keep from speaking the words even though she knew it might make the woman angry again.

"See it your way," the old woman replied as she began to thump her way across her kitchen floor. "That's your right, I guess. But I have rights, too. And I choose to have nothing to do with Him."

Anna felt her shoulders sag. What more could she—should she say?

❧   ❧   ❧

It was fall before the vacant lot was finally ready for the children of the area. Anna hoped for a long, warm autumn so that they might take advantage of it. But instead an early storm buried the sandbags that marked the ball diamond bases, and snow piled in drifts on the new sandbox.

"If folks hadn't been so slow in giving a hand," complained Anna, "the town youngsters could have had weeks of play before the snow came."

Austin nodded. Anna's idea had been a good one. Folks had taken a while to respond but had finally caught the vision. Help gradually came for the cleanup, and funds were raised by a community picnic and pie social so that simple equipment could be purchased.

But that wasn't the most rewarding result. The gang of boys had gradually softened toward the young preacher. They had stopped teasing and tormenting and had even dropped around toward the end of the project to lend a hand with the work. When they played their first ball game, Austin made sure that he was on hand, and they had invited him to be their pitcher.

The town as well had warmed toward the young minister.

"Real carin' fella," folks were saying. "Not just out to fill the offering plate on Sunday. Really wants to be of help to the community."

Two new families had been added to the church and they both cited the town playground project as the reason for their interest. Anna was pleased with the nice things that she heard said about her husband. She was sure God would use the goodwill to open doors for further ministry.

"Well, at least the playground will be all ready for use next spring," Anna stalwartly announced to her husband. And the young couple threw themselves into the work of the church and community.

❧   ❧   ❧

As soon as the snowdrifts disappeared and the spring puddles began to dry, the new playground became a hive of activity, just as Anna predicted. There were days when Austin might have wished he had never encouraged the project, for it was hard to concentrate on studying with the shouts and laughter from the vacant lot. Anna would only smile. She was glad that the children had a place to play so they wouldn't be looking for trouble to ease their boredom.

As she watched them play, her thoughts turned to the possibility of a garden.

"If only I had my own garden," she told herself for the hundredth time.

But there was no room to spade up even the

smallest of gardens on the little plot of ground sur-
rounding the parsonage. Anna nearly despaired
and then began to make her need a matter of
prayer.

Just as she was about to give up, Mrs. Landers,
one of the new parishioners, approached her one
Sunday.

"I was wondering if you might be interested in
having a garden, Mrs. Barker. Or would it be too
much trouble for you? I have more garden area than
I aim to plant. My arthritis limits me, you know."

Anna's eyes began to shine. The Landers' farm,
on the edge of town, was within easy walking distance.

"Oh, I'd be so pleased to have a spot," she joy-
fully answered the woman, while inwardly she
breathed a prayer of thankfulness. God had been
faithful—and in time, too. The spring weather was
perfect for the planting of a garden.

❧　　❧　　❧

"Well, we aren't any closer to having a church
building," Austin said one evening as they had
their supper.

Anna pushed the familiar and rather boring
stew around on her plate; then raised her eyes.
"Well, we can't be any further away," she ventured.

Austin looked puzzled.

Anna shrugged. "I just mean if we are ever going
to have a church here, each day that passes must
bring us closer to it," observed Anna.

Austin smiled, but Anna felt that it was forced.

"I, being human, would like to see a bit of evidence," he admitted.

"Well, we have a 'bit,'" said Anna, holding up her finger and thumb and making a very small measure.

Austin still looked puzzled.

"The building fund," she reminded him.

"The building fund amounts to about sixteen dollars," he responded. "We couldn't buy a bucket of nails with that."

"Well, it's a *bit*," insisted Anna.

Austin sighed. "I still think it would help the congregation to grow if we actually worshiped in a church building," he said. "Maybe we've been going about it the wrong way. Maybe we shouldn't have been waiting. Perhaps God expected us to get out and get busy. Look at the playground. Folks didn't think we were really serious about that until they started to see some action."

Anna nodded and pushed back her plate. She fleetingly wished she'd had ingredients for custard or a rice pudding.

"What do you think we should do?" she asked her husband.

"I don't know. Maybe make a bit more noise about it. Let folks know that the town needs a church."

"I think we might have used up the last vacant lot to make a playground," remarked Anna a little guiltily.

Austin's face sobered. "I hadn't thought of that. The playground location would be ideal," he admitted. At the look on Anna's face, he added, "There must be other suitable lots."

"Not in town," said Anna, shaking her head. "None that are the right location—and big enough. I walked the full length and breadth of it one day, and I couldn't find a one. Closest land is the Landers farm. One might get a small corner of that."

"That's too far out," said Austin. "It would be inconvenient for the older ones or small children who had to walk."

Anna agreed.

"What we really need is something right in the heart of town," went on Austin.

"Like the playground," observed Anna.

"The playground would be good," agreed Austin.

"But we aren't going to ask for it back, are we?" pushed Anna.

She thought it would be such a shame to give it to the children, and then take it from them again.

"A church is more important than a playground," reasoned Austin.

Anna reached out to place a hand on her husband's arm. "Do you see how it would look?" she said softly. "If you were to go to the town now and ask for the land for a church, everyone would think that was what you had in mind in the first place. That it was just—just a sneaky way to maneuver to get what you wanted. We can't do that, Austin. We just can't."

They sat in silence for a moment. Anna could see the muscles working in Austin's jaw and knew he was struggling with the problem.

"You're right," he said at last, giving her hand a squeeze. "We can't ask for it back. We'll have to trust God to give us something else."

❧   ❧   ❧

They were having their daily devotions together
when there was a thumping on the kitchen door
that Anna had come to recognize as Mrs. Paxton's
cane. She excused herself with a glance at Austin
and hastened to answer before the knocking could
come again.

"Yes, Mrs. Paxton," she said with a smile. "Come
on in."

"Didn't come to chatter," said the crusty old
woman, but before Anna could make further comment she continued.

"Heard you've been looking for a building for
your church."

"Yes," nodded Anna, "we have."

Mrs. Paxton shoved a piece of paper toward
Anna. "This here's the deed to the building I own
yonder," she said with a nod of her head. "You can
have it."

Anna was aware that Austin had risen to his
feet. "But—" he began.

Anna knew the condition of the building. She
also knew what Austin had in mind for the church.
The two did not correspond in any fashion. Anna
feared that Austin might make some comment of
refusal.

She turned to send her husband a silent message, then faced the woman with a delighted smile
as her hand reached for the proffered deed.

"That is most kind of you, Mrs. Paxton," she said
with sincerity. "My husband and I—and the entire
congregation—appreciate your generous offer."

Before Anna could say more, Mrs. Paxton had

turned and was going down the walk. As she went, Anna's eyes filled with tears.

When she finally shut the door and turned to face her husband, she could read protest in his stance and expression.

"Anna," he said, "that building is totally worthless."

"It must not be *totally* worthless," said Anna, lifting up the piece of paper. "No one ever put 'nothing' on paper."

"But it's falling down. It will take far more work than—"

"It's right in the heart of town," Anna said softly.

"I know it's a great lot, but the building itself is nothing but—"

"Maybe God wants us to fix it."

"We don't have the money to fix it. Don't you see . . . it would cost as much to fix that old pile of rotting boards as it would to build a new building."

"What I see," said Anna, fingering the piece of paper, "is that God has performed a miracle. To date, the whole town has been trying to get Mrs. Paxton to sell that building . . . or at least to rent or fix it up. She has constantly refused. Now here we are with the deed to a choice piece of property right in the middle of town. Right where you dreamed of the church standing. Wouldn't you call that a miracle?"

Tears spilled over and ran down Anna's cheeks. She did not lift her hand to brush them away.

"It . . . seems like rather a miracle," Austin said quietly, "when you put it that way."

"And if God can perform one miracle," went on

Anna, "what's stopping Him from bringing us an-other?"

Austin swallowed. Anna could sense his inner struggle. She knew the condition of the old build-ing. It certainly didn't match the church of Austin's dreams. His plans. She knew that the building fund held only sixteen dollars. And she also knew that they were going to need a great deal of money—of faith—of acceptance—if that building was ever to make a church. She knew the miracle Austin had been praying for was a little "larger"—a cleaner, better, more acceptable miracle than the one that had just presented itself. She held her breath and offered up a quick prayer. She really couldn't blame Austin if he refused to recognize . . .

But he held out his arms to her and Anna quickly moved toward him.

"Oh, Anna," he said into her hair. She could hear tears in his voice.

They wept as they clung together. They would accept what God had offered, knowing that it could and would work for good. It was so exciting to be a part of God's plan. They wondered where the next miracle would come from.

Chapter Twelve

Building

On the following Sunday, Pastor Barker announced to his little flock that they had been presented with a deed for the property on Main Street.

The response varied from smiles to groans.

"I know it will take a lot of work," he said brightly, trying to project as much enthusiasm as he could.

"The work we might handle," spoke up Mr. Page. "But what about the material?"

For a brief moment Austin looked to Anna. She gave him a wee smile and a slight nod in encouragement.

"I don't have the answers," the pastor admitted. "All I know is that God miraculously has brought us a building. He knows what is needed better than we do. So, I expect that He'll provide."

"Amen," said someone from the back of the schoolroom, and there were answering "Amens."

"Have you looked it over?" asked Mr. Brady.

"No," admitted Austin. "I thought that the board should make an inspection together."

Anna wondered if Austin needed moral support when he assessed the property. One man alone might stagger with the enormity of the task.

"Well, I guess we best get to it," said Mr. Brady.
"You fellows free tomorrow afternoon?"

There were nods from the other two members of
the board.

"That all right with you, Pastor?" asked Mr.
Brady, and Austin nodded in agreement.

"About three o'clock then," said Mr. Brady, the
board chairman, and the unofficial meeting was
considered dismissed.

⚜   ⚜   ⚜

It was even worse than they had guessed. Anna
could read it in Austin's face when he returned from
the tour of assessment.

"It's pretty bad, eh?" she offered.

Austin nodded without speaking.

Anna poured him a cup of weak coffee.

"Is there a starting place?" she prompted.

"Fellows don't even know where to start. The
logical place, of course, is the roof. No use doing
anything else until the roof is fixed. But the roof is
going to be one of the most costly projects. I don't
know where we'll ever find the money."

Anna waited until he had taken a couple sips of
the coffee.

"You don't suppose the community would help?"
she asked quietly.

Austin shook his head. "We haven't managed to
stir up much interest in the community," he reminded her.

"Well, maybe this is a good way to do it. When
they see that we are serious—just as you said—
then maybe they will . . . well . . . back us."

Austin took another sip of coffee. "I don't know, Anna," he said. "Sometimes it is terribly discouraging."

Anna reached out to pat his hand.

"It is discouraging," she said. "But that doesn't mean it's impossible."

"We've been here over a year. We have gained two families . . . and no converts," Austin commented, sounding very soul-weary.

She sat down beside him at the table and pulled a small delicate plant toward them.

"Look at this," she said, her voice compelling. "Mrs. Paxton brought me one of her violets. Little Pink Bonnet." Anna smiled. "She named this one herself."

Anna reached out a finger to trace around a delicate flower.

"Now, you might just see a violet here," Anna went on. "A beautiful little violet. But I see a miracle. Another miracle. Mrs. Paxton is gradually opening up, Austin. Gradually letting herself 'feel' again after all those years of bitterness and pain.

"I don't know if I will ever be able to win her to faith in Jesus, but I do know that God has put her in my life for a reason. And that in itself is a miracle. The fact that one person, any person, is here on this earth at just the right time to reach out to another. To be that link—that special someone to somehow give one more opportunity to make things right with the Savior—that is a miracle. Only God could arrange that.

"And if God cares that much for old Mrs. Paxton with all her quirks and doubts and angry feelings, then how do we know how many other hearts He is working in—right now—through little things. Words. Actions. Even a rickety old building. Maybe it is just what we need to challenge our little congregation. To bring us together. To make this town and community realize that we are for real. That we are serious about our faith."

Anna didn't know if she had said too much. If she had said enough. But Austin reached out to put an arm around her shoulder.

"So where does your next miracle come from, my Little Encourager?" he asked her.

"I have no idea," replied Anna. "But it will be exciting to see it come."

❧   ❧   ❧

"Hear you got that old building of Mrs. Paxton's," Mr. Parks said to Anna the next time she was in the store.

She nodded, remembering his words about the condition of the building and the eyesore it was to the town.

"Mighty glad to hear that," he continued. "It will help the whole town to have that mess cleaned up."

Anna nodded, but her face became serious.

"I wish I could say that we'll soon have it cared for," she said evenly, "but I'm afraid it won't look much different for some while yet."

Mr. Park's expression grew serious.

"We'd like to fix it, of course," Anna quickly went on, "but as yet we don't have the money. My husband says there isn't much use starting until the roof is fixed, and that will be a costly item for such a small congregation."

"You don't have the workers?"

"Oh, our men are quite willing to give of their time. It's the money for the materials that we can't yet afford."

"So what do you plan to do?" asked the grocer.

Anna smiled. "Wait," she said with confidence. "Wait for another miracle."

"A miracle might take years," responded the storekeeper dourly.

"Perhaps," said Anna.

"But the town needs the building fixed now."

"Yes," Anna replied sweetly. "*Now* is when we'd like to have our church, too. But God will care for it—in His own time—in His own way."

⚜   ⚜   ⚜

Three days later there was a knock on the parsonage door. Austin was busy preparing his Sunday sermon, so Anna answered. To her surprise Mr. Parks and the town banker stood on her step.

"May we come in?" the storekeeper asked, a little smile playing about his lips.

"Of course," invited Anna. "Please sit down. May I get you a cup of coffee?"

"No, no, we won't be staying long."

Austin came from his books at the sound of the voices. He greeted the men and repeated Anna's invitation, but Mr. Parks waved aside his offer.

"We had a special meeting of the town council last night," he explained. "That old store has been a concern of all the businessmen for years. We are anxious to have it fixed up. We decided that if it was the roof that was holding things up, we'd best do something about it."

He stopped to clear his throat and smiled more broadly.

"We aren't too good on waiting on God's miracles," he said with a nod toward Anna. "So we decided that we'd better take some action on our own."

He looked directly at Austin. "Your wife said that you have men who'll do the work—if the materials are provided. That right?"

Austin nodded.

"Well, we town businessmen have each put some money in the pot to cover the cost of materials. Once it's fixed up on the outside, we don't much care what you do on the inside."

Anna heard Austin take a deep breath.

"When can you start?" the banker was asking.

"I'll call a meeting just as soon as I can get out the word," responded Austin.

The banker nodded. "Come see me as soon as you make your arrangements. The money is on deposit at my bank."

Austin nodded again. Anna fought against the impulse to run to his side.

Mr. Parks stepped back. His face held a wide grin now. He made as though to replace his hat, and Anna knew he was preparing for departure.

"So you see, Mrs. Barker," he said, his eyes full on Anna's flushed face, "I guess we won't be needin' to stand around and wait on your God for that miracle, after all."

"No. No," said Anna, her hand going up to her warm cheek. "We won't have to wait. He's already performed it!"

For one moment Mr. Parks looked taken aback—and then his surprise turned to a chuckle. It seemed that the joke was on him.

❧   ❧   ❧

Anna's garden had been hard work, but it was worth it. The vegetables were doing nicely. Already they had enjoyed radishes, lettuce, beet greens, early onions, and a first picking of peas. Anna could hardly wait until the beans were ready—and then the turnips, carrots, and new potatoes. Each time she hoed she could taste the goodness still ahead.

As the summer wore on the work became more difficult and tiring.

"You shouldn't be in the sun," Mrs. Paxton scolded, but Anna smiled and assured her that she was fine.

"Your man should be doing the hoeing," insisted Mrs. Paxton.

Anna thought of Austin. Every minute he could spare was spent in working on the church building.

"The pastor is anxious to get the building rain-proofed," Anna reminded her neighbor.

Mrs. Paxton only nodded. She had been keeping a close eye on the progress down the street.

"Looks like they almost got it done," she said to Anna.

"Yes," Anna agreed, "but it is slow work. My husband has to work alone now. All the others had to get to their haying."

"You're working too hard—both of you," the woman surprised Anna by declaring.

"Well," said Anna, "it shouldn't be for much longer now."

❧   ❧   ❧

It seemed to Anna that it had been years and years since she had seen her family. She knew Austin would love to take her home, but there was no reasonable conveyance and no money for train fare.

Anna did not even mention the fact that she felt so homesick that at times she feared she might be ill. Instead, she prayed daily that God would help her through another day. But, oh, how she missed them. Especially her mother. If only she could see her. Could have a chat. Could see for herself that her mother was managing without her help. Anna dared not let herself dream of the possibility.

But Austin must have known the beat of Anna's heart. He must have sensed her loneliness, her desire for a visit with the woman who knew her better than anyone else in the world.

"What would you think of taking a little trip?" he asked her one morning at breakfast.

Anna raised her head from her bowl of oatmeal.

"I thought you might like to go home for a few days," Austin continued.

Anna tried to keep the excitement from her eyes. It sounded too good to be true.

"How?" she asked simply.

"By train."

"Oh, Austin. We couldn't afford the tickets. Could we?"

Anna felt both tremendous excitement and nagging doubt.

"No. Not we. But I think we could manage one."

Anna was quick to cut in. "One? But I couldn't—couldn't just—just go alone. I mean—I couldn't leave you here to—"

Austin reached for her hand, a smile erasing the tension that Anna often saw in his face.

"You think I've forgotten how to batch?" he teased.

"Oh, but I—"

"Why not? You need the trip. Your folks must miss you dreadfully. And I'm sure you miss them. I was hoping to work it out so that we both could go, but that doesn't seem . . ." Austin let the words trail away as he reached his free hand to pass his fingers through his hair and then massage the back of his neck.

"I have managed to squirrel away a bit," he confessed. "I'm sure that it will cover your ticket with no problem."

"But you—"

"I'll be fine," assured Austin, leaning forward to cup her chin in his hand and look directly into her eyes. "I will miss you terribly but I'll manage . . . for a few days."

Then he added in a lighter note, "I'll grant you five days, no more."

Anna wanted so much to see her family. But at the expense of being away from Austin? She wondered if the price was too high.

But the plans were laid, the ticket purchased, and Anna was soon on her way.

She enjoyed the trip in spite of herself. It was so good to see her mama again. So wonderful to have a warm hug from her father. So exciting to see how all of her brothers had grown. But especially good to sit at the kitchen table, sipping from one of her mother's cherished teacups just as though she were company, and have a heart-to-heart chat, a reminder that she was a beloved daughter.

When the time was up, Anna returned to the small town and the little parsonage, ready to go on with her chosen life.

Chapter Thirteen

Trouble

The din from the nearby playground was almost deafening at times. Anna sometimes wondered why they had to make so much noise just playing a game of ball. But she always reminded herself that she was glad they had a place to play.

So far none of the boys had joined them at the Sunday service, as she and Austin had hoped. It was true that they were no longer in as much trouble, though they still played occasional pranks on unsuspecting townspeople. And Anna even caught them mistreating a poor animal from time to time. But for the most part, the majority of their activities took place on the playing field. They had already worn out a number of balls and bats.

They weren't exactly pals with Austin or Anna, but they were no longer hostile either. So perhaps a little headway had been made. But it seemed that it was such a small amount of progress.

Anna often contemplated further ways that they could be reached. Especially the two from the family on the edge of town. She feared that unless a change was made in their lives, they would end up in serious trouble of some nature.

One day as Anna turned to lift pans of fresh-baked bread from her oven, there was a terrible crash from the back of the house. "Oh no!" she exclaimed, stopping mid-stride at the unmistakable sound of splintering window glass.

She placed the bread on the waiting board and went to the bedroom to view the damage. Glass was all over the bed and the floor. Very little was left in the window.

Anna felt like crying. There was no money to repair a broken window. There was barely enough to buy the necessary groceries each week. If it weren't for her garden, she didn't know if she could have made the pennies stretch.

There was no use fussing. Tears wouldn't repair the shattered glass. Anna looked out at the playground. Not a soul was in sight.

I guess they've all run and hidden, thought Anna. *I suppose they fear our wrath.*

Anna picked the ball off the bedroom floor and went in search of the boys.

By the time she reached the vacant lot, heads were appearing from behind small bushes. When they saw her coming, they quickly disappeared again.

"Boys," she called. "Tommy? I found your ball. I thought you might need it to finish your game."

Anna stood with the ball in hand, peering at the hiding places.

At length a head peeked out from a shrub, then another, and soon sheepish faces were appearing.

"Your ball," said Anna, holding out the small white sphere. "I figured you wouldn't be able to finish your game without it."

Tommy Fallis was the first to make full appearance. He moved slowly toward her.

"Accidents happen," said Anna, remembering when her brother Will had broken a window at home.

Tommy accepted the proffered ball. He still seemed unable to believe that she wasn't going to lash out at them for the mishap.

But Anna gave him a smile, and then turned to smile at the heads poking over the bushes. "Have fun," she called out to them, then turned and walked back to her house.

Anna went to work cleaning up the mess. She cut her finger on a sliver of glass in the process and had to stop to put on a makeshift bandage. Then she set to work again.

The afternoon sun was warm overhead and the flies buzzed lazily in the shimmering heat. In no time they decided that they'd rather be in than out, and Anna saw them making entrance through the broken window.

Anna did not care for flies in her house. She knew she had to do something quickly, so she got one of her tea towels and tacked it into the window frame. It wouldn't do anything at all about the weather, but at least it should keep the flies from her kitchen.

✢   ✢   ✢

It seemed to Anna that it rained every day for two weeks during August. But that was an exaggeration. Over and over she and Austin expressed to each other their thankfulness that the new church building was waterproof.

143

Anna had tried to make her bedroom just as watertight by tacking cardboard over the broken window. Each time the rain soon soaked through, the paper became soggy and the wall began to drip.

Austin took over then, borrowing pieces of board from the church project. Even that did not keep out the water. It seeped through every seam, running down the already stained wall and making puddles on the floor. Anna found herself wiping it up several times a day when it rained.

When there was a break in the clouds, Anna felt she must do something different.

Maybe if I make a heavy paste and patch the seams, she thought. *If it has a chance to dry, it might hold out the water.*

Anna worked quickly with her flour and water mixture. In the west she could see clouds beginning to form again. She hurried outside and began to smear it heavily wherever there was a join of boards.

The nearby playground had not been used for a number of days. It was too soggy, with big puddles where the bases should be. Anna noticed the quiet as she worked with her paste.

I rather miss the noise, she admitted to herself. *At least it was a happy sound. I would rather have it than the drip, drip of rain.*

"There," she said aloud, stepping back to observe her handiwork. "Maybe that will keep out the water."

Then Anna shifted her eyes to the skies. "If it just has time to dry properly."

Anna picked up her smeary paste pot and returned to her kitchen.

The paste managed to dry before the next rain. For the first few hours Anna thought her idea had worked, but the steady rain gradually washed away her paste, and Anna was back to wiping floors again.

The rain finally did cease to fall and things began to dry out. Anna asked Austin to remove the boards from the window so she could clean up the casement. But they were kept handy in case they had to hastily be tacked in position again.

What will we ever do when winter comes? Anna wondered.

They had been making an effort to save enough to buy new window glass, but there were only a few pennies in the cup. It had once reached eighty-six cents and then Mr. Perkins, an elderly bachelor across the street, had taken ill. Anna had borrowed from her little savings to buy enough ingredients for a nourishing soup.

And now they were down to pennies again.

There was a knock on the door and Anna crossed to answer, tying her apron around her small frame as she did.

A cluster of boys stood on her step. Anna recognized them as the "gang."

"We brung the money for the window," said the biggest one of the lot, extending a grimy hand filled with coins.

Anna's eyes widened. "Where ever did you get all that money?" she gasped, doubt in her eyes.

"We worked fer it," one of the boys replied.

"We saw you tryin' to fix the hole," volunteered Tommy Fallis.

"We figured the rain must still be comin' in."

Anna nodded. She was beginning to regain her composure. She even managed a smile.

"Come in," she invited, stepping aside.

They came in, pushing together like a herd of sheep. The biggest boy still held the coins in his hand.

"I'm sorry, I don't have enough chairs," said Anna, "but some of you may sit on the floor."

Anna wished she had cookies. They hadn't had cookies in the house for ever so long.

"Would you like a slice of bread and jam?" she offered and saw several heads nod. One of the boys even dared to say, "Um-m-m."

Anna hurried to prepare the bread. There was a bit of whispering and shifting as the boys huddled on her kitchen floor.

"Now," said Anna. "I know some of you—but not all. Could you tell me your names, please?"

They held back at first, and then all gave their names at once.

"One at a time," laughed Anna. "We'll start with Tommy Fallis here on the end."

"Robert Collins," said the boy next to Tommy. Anna noted his freckled face. He shouldn't be hard to remember.

"Sid Cross," said the one who still clutched the coins.

A-ha, thought Anna. *From the house on the edge of town.*

The next boy spoke without looking up from his clasped hands, "Ben Cross."

A brother, thought Anna.

"Paul Gillis," said the next boy. Anna had never seen Paul with the gang before.

"Are you new in town, Paul?" she stopped the proceedings to ask.

"No," he answered, shifting uncomfortably.

"His ma's away," offered Tommy as though that explained his presence.

"I see," said Anna as she spread jam on the last piece of bread.

Then she turned to the final boy in the cluster. "Your name?"

"Carl," he said nervously, without a glance upward.

"And your last name, Carl?" asked Anna innocently as she piled the slices onto a plate for serving.

Tommy began to snicker and several others joined him, elbowing one another and pushing with bodies. The boy blushed and hung his head.

"It's Carl," piped up Paul Gillis.

"Oh," said Anna, without looking at the squirming group. "Your last name is Carl. And your first?"

There was a real outbreak then.

"It's Carl, too," hooted Tommy.

Anna picked up the plate of bread and tried to keep her voice even. Inside she was thinking, *What parent would ever do a thing like that?* Outwardly she said softly as she began passing the slices from boy to boy, "Carl Carl. That is a most interesting name. An advantage, too. You only needed to learn to spell one." She smiled.

The hooting stopped. Anna wasn't sure if it was because of her comment or the bread slices that were quickly disappearing off the plate.

When she reached Sid, he indicated the money in his hand, and Anna knew he was telling her that he couldn't eat with his hand still full. She noticed the grime on his hands, and cringed. Then she remembered that she had seen her farm brothers eat with hands almost as dirty when not caught by her mother and they all had lived.

"The money," she said and extended her hand. "I want to hear about how you worked for all this money."

She laid the money on her table and finished passing out the bread.

"Now," she said as she put the empty plate back on the table, "how did you ever earn so much?"

"We told folks how—how we broke the window—and how you was havin' trouble keepin' out the rain—and asked if they had jobs—and they did," offered Tommy in a rush.

"Mr. Parks hired us the most," cut in Sid.

"Yeah," interposed Paul, "he said somethin' 'bout, 'Guess he might as well work another miracle,' or somethin'."

Anna smiled. Yes. Yes, it was another miracle. At the rate she had been able to save, they would have gone through a cold winter with the wind blowing off the Arctic into their bedroom.

"You don't know how much I appreciate what you have done," said Anna, her eyes shining. "In fact, I'm sure Pastor Barker would like to tell all the folks about your good deed. Let's see. Maybe— maybe a good time to do that would be next Sunday. Right at the school. We still meet there every Sunday, you know. We could have you all in the very first row and then when he tells the folks about you, you can all stand up."

Eyes were sparkling, elbows were working. Only Carl hung his head.

"How does that sound?" asked Anna.

"I don't have any special Sunday clothes," spoke up Paul.

"Neither do I," said Tommy.

"That's fine," Anna hurried to assure them. "People don't go to the service to look at clothes. We will be looking at your faces." Then she quickly added to keep the focus on the faces, "So make sure they are scrubbed and clean . . . and your hair slicked down."

There was a scramble as they rose to leave. Anna heard excited chattering as they went down her walk. She closed her eyes and prayed. Then turned back to the kitchen.

"I wonder. . . ?" she mused as she lifted the empty plate from the table.

Then her eyes moved to the little pile of coins, and eagerly her fingers reached out to sort and count. There was enough. Just enough for a pane of glass. Anna had already asked Mr. Parks the price. How strange that it should be exact.

And then Anna smiled. No, it wasn't strange at all. Hadn't Mr. Parks himself hired the boys the most? Who better than the store owner would know the price of a windowpane?

Anna scooped up the coins and let them drop one

by one into her "savings" cup. When Austin came home for his supper, she would have some good news for him.

❧ ❧ ❧

The next Sunday all the boys but Carl were seated in the front row, their faces scrubbed clean, their hair slicked back—and their clothes as dirty and rumpled as usual.

But Anna noticed little except the shiny faces. She was so glad to see them that the tears filled her eyes.

Austin made much of the good deed of the boys and they blushed and beamed by turn.

Three of them were back the following Sunday. Then two—then back up to four. Their attendance was sporadic—but they were coming. Anna thanked the Lord for that.

"I think Mr. Parks might have been involved in a miracle that he wasn't counting on," she mused. "What else would have ever brought those boys to our service?"

And suddenly, all of those messy puddles on her floor, the unsightly stains on her walls, and the misery of the days of fighting rain seemed a small price to pay.

Chapter Fourteen

Sorrow

"Anna. There's bad news."

Anna stopped the swing of the garden hoe and looked at her husband. His face was flushed and he was breathing heavily as though he had run all the way to the farm garden. Her face turned pale, her eyes widened. Her first thought was of her mother.

"Why don't you sit down?" Austin offered, easing the hoe from her hands and casting a look around them.

Anna's eyes followed his. There was no place to sit except on the ground.

"What is it?" she managed.

"Shouldn't you—?"

"Tell me," cut in Anna, her voice raising with her fear. "Tell me. Is it Mama?"

Austin had his arm about her as he eased her toward the grass at the side of the garden.

"No. No," he said quickly. "It isn't any of your family."

The garden was still not totally dry after all the rain. Anna had to watch as she walked so she wouldn't misstep and end up with muddy shoes. She skirted a small patch of mud that almost took her out of Austin's arms.

"It's little Timmy Lawes," continued Austin and Anna felt her throat constrict. Little Timmy was her favorite. Such a beautiful child. So warm and loving. Such a delight to hold and cuddle. Whenever Anna scooped him up onto her lap, she thought ahead to the delight of having her own baby.

"Is he sick?" she managed, the fear back in her voice again.

"There was an accident," said Austin, stopping to look into her face—to will her his strength. "He's gone."

For a moment Anna stood where she was. Her face drained of color, her hands fluttered to her breast. Slowly she shook her head. "No," she denied. "No. There must be some mistake."

She felt her legs trembling beneath her and moved to lean more heavily on her husband.

"No," she said again.

"It was a drowning," explained Austin. "You know how full all the ditches are with all the rain. Cal found him."

"No." One last denial before the tears came.

Then her thoughts turned from her own shock to that of the young parent. "Poor Cal. Poor Cal."

Anna began to sob and Austin pulled her close and held her, his face buried in her hair.

They went to the Lawes as soon as they could change from their work clothes and hitch the team. All the way to the farm home Anna's thoughts were on the grieving family.

Oh, God, she prayed over and over, *if ever Austin needed a real minister's wife, it's now. If only—if only I knew what to say and what to do.*

Anna felt painfully inadequate for the task before them. How could she, a mere farm girl, inexperienced and untrained, possibly bring comfort to the grieving mother?

"Oh, God," she moaned again and again. "Oh, God."

It was not an easy day—for anyone. The young mother was in shock and went from mourning her baby to screams of denial. "You're lying," Mandy kept accusing her distraught husband. "Everyone is lying. He's just sleeping. See. See. He's sucking his thumb just like he always does in his sleep. He's just sleeping."

The tiny boy's thumb was nowhere near his mouth.

And then the next minute the stricken mother would be rocking back and forth, the tears falling as she moaned and sobbed, "Oh, my baby. My poor little lost baby. Why did it have to be you? Why did it have to be you?"

Everyone was relieved when she finally fell into an exhausted sleep.

Anna busied herself in the farm kitchen. Others had to be cared for. Shocked siblings had to be fed. Held. Comforted. The day was a living nightmare for them. Anna ached to be able to help but could only cradle them close and assure them they were loved.

She and Austin stayed the night. He feared they might be needed. He was right. The mother awoke from time to time and cried for her baby. Anna held her in her arms and spoke words of love and comfort while her heart prayed that God would intervene on the grieving mother's behalf.

By morning Anna felt as numb as the young

mother looked. Charles stumbled about as a blind man, trying to be strong for the sake of his grieving spouse and crying family.

"We need to make plans," he said to Austin over a cup of Anna's strong coffee.

Austin nodded. "I'll do whatever I can," he assured Charles.

Anna left the two at the kitchen table. She didn't think she was up to hearing the details for the funeral service. She took a cup of tea to Mandy, hoping she would be able to coax the woman to take a few sips of the beverage.

In the afternoon they left, taking the children with them. Anna had debated the wisdom of removing the little ones from the home. Did they need their own parents at such an hour—even though the couple was unable to give them the care and support they so desperately needed? Or would it be better to take them from the heavy grief that hung about the home? Anna wasn't sure. But Austin suggested it to the parents and they nodded a mute consent. The children didn't argue the fact either, and even seemed to brighten as the journey progressed.

Perhaps this is the right thing to do, Anna decided.

But when night came and it was time to tuck the children into the bed that had been prepared on the living room floor, Anna had cause to wonder again. It took her hours to still the fears, dry the tears, and bring comfort to little people who wanted to go home.

৬৬৬   ৬৬৬   ৬৬৬

They had the funeral service two days later. The community came in full support. Anna wept as she saw the family clinging together on the backless bench. Mandy was so pale that Anna feared the distraught mother might pass out during the service. It seemed that the only thing holding her upright was her husband's arms. The children nestled as close to their parents as they could press their little bodies. Anna was glad that Austin kept the service short. She wasn't sure they would have been able to endure much longer.

The small casket was lowered into the still-damp ground. Anna thought she saw water in the bottom of the dark hole—and she cringed. She prayed that Mrs. Lawes had not noticed it. It was a cruel reminder of the cause of this death.

"Please—come to the house and I'll fix tea," Anna invited, and the family followed her, still clinging together.

Anna knew they were facing some very difficult months ahead.

❧   ❧   ❧

The new building was finally ready for occupancy. The dedication was set for the fifteenth of October, Anna made little announcement posters and Austin tacked them up around town. The whole community was invited to the service, and some new faces did appear among the little crowd.

Anna had delivered a personal invitation to Mrs. Paxton. "After all, it's your building," Anna reminded the lady who stood frowning at the invitation in Anna's outstretched hand.

"Not mine. Yours," she replied crossly. "I have nothing at all to do with it anymore."

"But it was your kindness—" began Anna.

"Kindness don't amount to ker-doodle," interrupted Mrs. Paxton. "Got the rest of the town off my back—that's what."

Anna didn't turn to cross the street to her own little home until the door had closed firmly in her face.

Anna tried to put the incident behind her on the day of dedication. There was so much to think about—pleasant things: Austin, the guests, the service. The church ladies even served coffee and sandwiches afterward. In all, it was a rather gala celebration. The district superintendent and his wife, along with a few other church dignitaries, came for the occasion.

"You should have seen the building we started with," boasted Mr. Brady. "Pastor never thought we'd make anything of it, I reckon—but then he just put his mind and his back to work—and look what we got now!"

Anna beamed as she looked at her husband. His dream had come true. Largely by his own sweat and his own two hands, he had his church building.

"My husband has put in many hours," Anna acknowledged, her eyes shining with pride.

The superintendent nodded in appreciation. "He's to be highly commended," he agreed.

Anna felt that her cup was brimming, threatening to spill over. And then a shadow fell across her thinking. *Now that we have a real church, folks will expect me to be a real minister's wife—and I have no idea how to go about it.*

The troubling thought nearly spoiled the rest of the day for Anna.

Chapter Fifteen

Concerns

"Any comments on last Sunday's sermon?" Austin asked one Saturday afternoon.

Anna looked up from her Bible. She was preparing for the Sunday school lesson. Mr. Brady was the teacher, but Anna liked to have background for the lesson. Rarely did she have the courage to speak out in class, but Mr. Brady had the unnerving habit of calling upon her. Anna wished to be prepared. Also, for her own enrichment, Anna liked to study so that she could glean all that was possible from the lessons.

"I thought you handled that somewhat difficult scripture well," Anna responded to Austin's question.

"I worry," said Austin. "I worry about balance. Does it have enough depth—yet is it stated simply enough so even the younger members of the congregation will understand it?"

Anna cocked her head and considered his comment. Certainly she had understood the message, and she had no special knowledge or training.

"I followed it easily enough and yet—"

"But you have a quick mind," Austin reminded her. "And you have done considerable study."

His words surprised Anna. She didn't feel that her mind was comprehending all it should, and she certainly hadn't had opportunity to study in any formal fashion.

"Does it have depth?" went on Austin. "Did you gain any new insights—learn any new truths?"

Anna's mind quickly reviewed the sermon. Yes. She had learned about the culture of the early Israelites. She had gained knowledge about the laws given in Deuteronomy. Understanding the laws and the reason for their existence helped her to gain a clearer picture of the God of the Hebrews. Her God.

"Yes," she answered, feeling a little quickening of her pulse. "Yes—in fact, I got quite excited over the third point. That God placed all the people on the same plane. That the rich were not to bring any more for their offering, nor the poor any less. It is wonderful to realize that people cannot buy their way into favor, or that less possessions means a lower-class citizen.

"And I liked the way you carried it into the New Testament and Christ's provision for mankind. The same blood was shed for all. Rich or poor. Male or female. Jew or Gentile. Yes, I was moved."

Austin nodded. "And you feel it is clear enough for the younger, the less knowledgeable to understand?"

Anna thought carefully. The sermon had developed and progressed step by step. Each point building on the other, proceeding forward, clearly, yet concisely. It was well planned. Well done. Austin was a good preacher.

"Yes. Yes, I saw no problems," Anna answered truthfully.

She knew Austin counted on her for honesty—not for flattery.

"Good," said Austin simply. Anna's comments seemed to be enough. He lifted his hat from the wall peg and prepared to leave.

"I'm going over to work at the church. Shouldn't be long."

Anna nodded, then watched the back of her husband disappear out the door.

It was several minutes before she could get her attention back to the study of the book of Acts. Her thoughts kept swinging back to Austin.

He *was* a good preacher. His message for Sunday was exciting, thought-provoking, yet simple enough to be understood. Anna was sure there were those in attendance who could benefit from the sermon. But would they? Anna's thoughts particularly focused on a row of teenage girls. There were five in the group. Anna had been praying for them continually over the months they had been at the church. None of them seemed to have much spiritual interest. Anna worried about them.

It wasn't that they ignored the young preacher. On the contrary, they seemed to be most attentive to Austin. But to the man, not the message. Just to watch the girls was a reminder to Anna that she had married a most attractive young man. They tittered and giggled and poked and squirmed and tried to get personal attention.

If only they would sit still and listen. Really listen, thought Anna, *then perhaps the Word of God would have a chance to root and bear fruit.*

But the girls did not sit quietly, did not listen, did not seem at all concerned with the condition of their souls. They were much more intent on coaxing a smile from the preacher or receiving his hearty handshake.

Austin seemed totally oblivious to the commotion he stirred, but Anna felt inner concern. Surely the rest of the congregation noticed. Did they feel that Austin encouraged the action? Did they share Anna's concern for the spiritual well-being of their daughters? Or did they simply consider it a harmless phase of growing up? One that gave them, as parents, no concern and should give Anna no concern either? Anna did not know.

She prayed over the matter. She didn't feel that she really could discuss it with Austin. If he was unaware of the situation, she did not want to make him uneasy by drawing it to his attention. That would make his ministry cramped—difficult. Anna chose to ignore the giggles as much as possible, but to be quietly on hand so that no false rumors had opportunity to circulate.

But oh, how she wished that the truth of Austin's preaching would become as important to the five young ladies as a bit of attention from the young preacher seemed to be.

❧   ❧   ❧

"We are to have a new parishioner," Austin said as he hung his hat on the wall peg. Anna heard the excitement in his voice and turned to rejoice with him.

"She dropped by the church this morning and asked concerning the time of service," went on Austin.

"Wonderful!" responded Anna, hoping with all her heart that it was Mrs. Paxton.

"She is just making the move to town," he continued, and Anna was disappointed. It wasn't Mrs. Paxton, after all.

"Her name is Mrs. Larkins."

"Where is she from?" asked Anna.

"She's moving out from Calgary. She grew up here, married, and moved to Calgary. Now that she has been widowed, she has decided to move back home—even though she no longer has family here."

Anna's mental images tumbled over one another in quick succession. The word *widowed* had fostered many of them. She pictured an older woman, alone—desolate—lonely—without family. Anna determined to make the acquaintance of the widow immediately so that she might offer her friendship.

"Where does she live?" she asked.

"She won't be arriving until next Thursday. I promised to get a couple of men to help unload her furniture and get her settled."

Anna was pleased with Austin's foresight.

"She will be moving into the Lungren house," Austin said in answer to her question.

Anna knew the house. It had been vacant for the past three months upon the death of the elderly Miss Lungren. It was, by far, the most elegant house in the little town. It would seem that the widow was not destitute.

"Are her children all grown?" asked Anna.

"She doesn't have children," responded Austin, and Anna felt the shiver of sympathy pass through her again.

"So she is all alone?"

"She does have a brother and his family in the area, but they haven't gotten on too well. Guess there was a rift there many years ago and it has never been healed."

Such a sad situation, thought Anna. Such a shame for family to forfeit a relationship over some distant misunderstanding. Again, Anna felt concern for the woman.

"I guess she'll need our help—and our prayers," she said simply and planned to do all she could to make the widow lady feel at home in their town and especially in their church.

❧   ❧   ❧

Austin spent three full days helping the new member get moved in and settled. A couple of the church men also gave a hand. Anna sent word and offered her assistance as well as invitations for meals, but was graciously though firmly turned down.

"There is no need for you to leave your more pressing duties," the widow's note of reply stated. "The menfolk will move things about. And I really must arrange things myself. But I thank you. And . . . I am on a very strict diet." Anna felt further concern for the poor little woman. She acknowledged with regret that the parsonage's simple provisions could not supply the needs of a strict diet.

So Anna held herself in check, determined not to intrude but to offer her friendship to the new member at the gathering in church on Sunday morning.

When it was time for the Sunday service, Anna

found her eyes quickly scanning the congregation as she settled herself onto the wooden bench. She saw no new face among the gathering.

The Sunday school hour passed and there was some stirring about as people resituated themselves for the morning worship service.

Still no new face appeared. Anna thought she sensed Austin watching the door as well.

They were well into the second hymn when Anna heard the door open. She knew she could not turn to see who had entered, but she guessed by the slight lifting of Austin's head and the barely perceptible nod, that it was their new member. It was all Anna could do to keep her eyes to the front. She even had difficulty concentrating on the morning sermon. A thing very rare—and disconcerting—for Anna.

Her mind kept wrestling with ways that she might offer friendship. A strict diet ruled out tea times or the deliveries of baked goods or even custards. And if the woman was frail and elderly, shared activities might be difficult. Anna worked the problem over and over and came no closer to a solution.

I guess I'll just have to offer "me." My friendship. I can think of nothing more, she finally concluded and forced her attention back to Austin's sermon about the Prodigal Son. Anna had read his sermon notes and liked his fresh approach to the old story. She had prayed that the five girls in the second row might listen carefully to the truths. But they seemed to be primping and flirting in their customary fashion. Anna slipped into prayer again.

When the service had ended, Austin stepped

from the platform and waited for Anna to proceed with him down the aisle. At long last Anna was able to openly look for their new parishioner. So intent was she in seeking out a wrinkled, troubled face that she almost bypassed the real Widow Larkins. In fact, when she did spot her, Anna was sure there must be some mistake. But Austin was stopping and gently prodding her toward the newcomer.

"Anna, I would like you to meet Mrs. Larkins," he was saying. "Mrs. Larkins, my wife, Anna Barker."

Anna found herself looking into two of the most intense blue eyes she had ever seen. They were framed by long dark lashes and set in a perfectly formed face, with creamy skin, slightly flushed cheeks, and full, red lips. Anna felt her own cheeks coloring. She had been so totally unprepared.

The young woman was lifting herself gracefully from the wooden bench and smiling sweetly— though her eyes were on the face of Austin, not on Anna.

Anna had opportunity to study the young woman further. Golden masses of curls were tucked tastefully beneath the brim of a powder blue, wide-brimmed bonnet with a large bow of deeper blue sweeping over the left side. The trim-fitting suit matched perfectly the color, while a white lacy jabot, with more frills than Anna would have felt possible to crowd onto a blouse front, softened the clean lines of the suit's cut. Anna's eyes followed the slim form all the way down to the dainty slippers that graced the narrow feet.

Her cheeks flushed even more. Never had she

seen such elegance. Never had she felt so plain and drab in comparison.

The new woman extended a white-gloved hand toward Anna, but her eyes were still on Austin.

"I am pleased to meet you," she murmured, then hurried on. "My, you are privileged indeed to have a husband with such knowledge of the Scriptures. Why, I just drank in every word. I have never, never received such—such insight into the story of the—the—that boy."

Her lashes swept down momentarily to rest against her smooth cheeks. Then they opened wide and her blue eyes fastened on Austin. "I am looking forward to the services—more than you'll ever know."

Anna stole a glimpse at Austin, wondering what his response would be to the open flattery. He smiled warmly and nodded his head. "We will be happy to have you in our congregation," he assured the newcomer. Then he turned to Anna, seemingly ignorant of the flirtation in the other woman's voice and manner. "Anna, would you be so kind as to introduce Mrs. Larkins to the ladies. I must get to the door to greet the people."

He walked away—just like that.

Anna blinked, then turned to Mrs. Larkins. The new woman seemed as confused as Anna. The coy smile quickly left her face, but she had manners enough to be friendly and gracious as Anna carried out Austin's request.

The young widow seemed to be aware of the small stir she caused wherever she went, and she soon was making the most of it. Anna quietly watched her. She certainly was a beautiful and poised woman. And she certainly was young to be a widow. Anna felt both sorry for her and frightened of her—all at the same time. She did hope the woman would feel at home in the little town. In the little church. And she did pray—with all her heart—that there wouldn't be trouble in store for her young and possibly naive husband.

Chapter Sixteen

Lessons

As the weeks slipped by, Mrs. Larkins still vied with the five teenage girls for Austin's attention. Her ways were much more subtle—much more refined than those of the youngsters—but Anna thought them to be just as obvious. She prayed that the congregation might not blame Austin for the overtures. Anna had seen no encouragement on Austin's part. Indeed, he seemed to be totally oblivious to what the woman was trying to do. Anna wondered about his naivety. But as long as Austin seemed unaware of the situation, Anna determined she would not draw it to his attention. To do so would only serve to make him sensitive and uncomfortable, she reasoned.

But what about the rest of the congregation? Anna was sure they had noticed the young widow's attempts to get special attention from the attractive youthful minister. Anna wasn't sure how to deal with thoughts and feelings from people that never came out into the open.

If someone would make comment to me, I could respond, she often thought. But as long as nothing was said, Anna dared not bring up the subject.

Yet Anna was nearly sure that plenty was being

said behind their backs. No one could be blind to the intent of the young widow. No one except Austin himself.

"Mrs. Larkins has asked me to check her furnace," Austin said one day as he finished up his dinner.

It was not the first of the things that Mrs. Larkins had asked Austin to check. Anna lifted her head, wondering again if she should speak out—if she should warn her husband how his little trips to the Larkins' abode might look to other people. So far, he had insisted that she, Anna, accompany him on his little visits, or he had invited one of the town boys as an opportunity to get closer by making him his "helper" for that excursion.

Anna was pleased with Austin's handling of the situation. She wasn't sure if he fully realized his own wisdom—but he had managed things wisely. *How is he going to deal with this request?* Anna wondered, and turned her eyes back to her plate.

"I said I'd send over Mr. Brady. He knows much more about furnaces than I do," continued Austin, and Anna could not help but shake her head in admiration and astonishment. Austin seemed so totally innocent.

"What she needs is a husband—a house full of kids," Austin remarked. "I think she is lonely—and bored. She doesn't seem to have the least idea of how to fill her days and hours. Now, if you were in her situation, you'd busy yourself with finding ways to reach out to others. And the extra minutes would be well used in reading. Enriching your mind. I can't possibly picture you with time on your hands. No matter what your circumstance."

Austin paused to take a long drink of his tea.

"But then," he continued in a matter-of-fact tone, "I don't think Mrs. Larkins is used to using her mind to any great extent."

Anna looked up in surprise.

Austin met her gaze evenly.

"Does it shock you that I criticize one of my flock? I guess I shouldn't—but this is just between you and me. I know it won't go beyond this table."

Austin paused only long enough to make eye contact with Anna.

"The woman is totally—totally incapable of thought beyond her fancy ribbons and bows. Shallow. A child is more perceptive."

"Austin!" said Anna softly, shock edging her voice.

"Well, it's true—and it might as well be said," he responded. "Do you know what she wanted the last time she called me over? *The clock set!* Can you imagine? The clock set. It was ten minutes out. She said that was why she is always late for church. But I noticed that after it was set, she was still late. Ben set it. I had him with me and he set it. Just a kid. Now, why couldn't she have set her own clock? It was as simple as moving the hands.

"You know what I think? I think she just wants attention. She's so bored—and so shallow that she has to dream up things. Why doesn't she get out and get involved? Get her thoughts off herself and onto someone else?"

Anna was tempted to respond. She could have said, *She has her thoughts on someone else. You!* But Anna did not say it. In a way she felt sorry for the woman. It looked as if all her coy attempts had been utterly unprofitable. Austin was still unaware of the woman's intention.

"Well, I've seen Martin Smith giving her the eye," went on Austin. "She would be well advised to pay a little attention to him. And Carl Falks. He's been dipping his hat and grinning. I think he is struck on her, too."

Anna too had seen the young men of the community watching the young widow with interest. In the case of Carl Falks, Anna could not fault Mrs. Larkins for failing to respond to the advances, but Martin Smith seemed like a fine young man.

"Maybe she is a bit fussy," responded Anna simply, aware that Mrs. Larkins really was reaching for the best—her Austin.

"Then maybe she would have been wiser to stay in the city," Austin responded as he pushed back from the table. "She might have had a wider selection there."

Anna nodded.

Austin leaned to give her a kiss. "Well, I'd better run on over to Brady's and see if he has time to look at that furnace—just in case something really is wrong with it," he said. Anna nodded. She had things she had to do, too. She needed to get the dishes out of the way.

When the door closed on Austin, Anna felt strange and mixed emotions. She puzzled over the fact that Austin still did not see what the widow obviously meant by her repeated calls for his help. She was glad Austin's male ego had not been flattered by the calls. She was glad his "calling" and his faith had kept him from possible trouble. But deep down inside, Anna felt concern and sympathy for the young widow. Surely she must be lonely and inwardly troubled to act as aggressively and openly as the woman did. It must be terribly hard on her self-esteem to be so totally ignored in all attempts to get personal attention. Anna took a few moments to pray before clearing the table.

※　　※　　※

"What would you think about a Christmas program?" Anna asked as she and Austin drove out for an afternoon call.

"We always have a Christmas service," he responded.

"Not a Christmas service—a Christmas program. For the children. You know, songs, recitations, a little play. Something to really involve all the children who come to the church—and any others who might be interested."

Austin nodded.

"There is nothing that draws people like the performance of their offspring," continued Anna. "And no better time to do a program than at Christmastime."

"The school always has one," Austin reminded her.

"Yes, and it is always well attended. And now that we have our own church, I think we could use the opportunity to draw a community crowd as well."

Austin seemed to be carefully considering her words.

"It's a lot of work," he said at last.

"Well, I'm willing to put time into it," responded Anna.

Inwardly she felt her lack of experience, of abilities, but she was willing to do all she could.

"Sounds like a good idea—if you feel up to it," Austin responded after further thinking.

Their first child was on the way and Anna had been feeling tired. But she tried to brush that aside.

"I—I wish I had someone to work with—someone with more knowledge about how to go about it," she admitted, "but I really don't know whom to ask."

"We could speak to the congregation on Sunday. See if there are any volunteers," offered Austin.

That sounded like a good idea to Anna. She felt that she would need all the help she could get.

❧   ❧   ❧

It turned out that there were no volunteers for the Christmas program, though everyone assured Anna they thought the idea a good one.

"I'm sure a number of the town children would be happy to take part," enthused Mrs. Brady. "We could put up some posters or pass out little invitations or something."

Anna decided to do both. Mr. Parks allowed her to put up an announcement in his store. "Guess it can't hurt anything," he had told Anna, and she carefully printed up her little sign and posted it in his front window.

Then Anna began to print up simple invitations to "join the fun and excitement of being part of the first annual Church Christmas Program" and handed them out up and down the streets.

She set the first meeting for practice for the third Thursday of November. Then she went to work looking for suitable material.

She found nothing that seemed to meet their needs, so she spent hours designing her own program, tying scripture and songs together and weaving in the story of the first Christmas. Austin reviewed the material and gave hearty approval.

"It has a great message—yet is wonderfully entertaining," he assured Anna, but she still had doubts. She knew nothing about writing scripts or recitations. She did hope that the material wouldn't be disjointed and meaningless.

She was disappointed with the turnout on the first afternoon of practice, but then for some reason the idea seemed to catch on. Soon there were twenty-two children, of varying ages, meeting at the small church. Anna assigned parts, sending them home for memorization. She had her hands more than full trying to keep the attention of everyone as the practicing progressed, but the program soon began to come together. The children seemed to be excited about putting it on for the community.

"We could have a good attendance," Austin informed Anna. "I hear comments wherever I go. People are looking forward to it."

"People always enjoy seeing their children perform," Anna reminded him, but she didn't admit the nervous twitches that assailed her when she thought forward to the night of the actual event. What if things went all wrong? What if people didn't understand her message? What if the children totally failed in their presentation? What if. . . ? Would it reflect poorly on Austin? On the church? Maybe she had been wrong to assume that she could handle such a task.

But Anna plunged on, trying with each practice to improve the presentation.

The date was set for the twenty-first of December. To Anna's amazement, the town seemed to be buzzing about the event. She did hope that she wouldn't let them down. The children had worked so hard, had been so faithful in practice. The stage was ready. The simple costumes were ready. Each part had been thoroughly memorized. Anna prayed daily that she would be able to carry out her part of directing the little presentation.

But on the twentieth, a storm swept through town. The howling winds and blowing snow soon made Anna realize that the country folks would surely not be able to get to town.

"We will be a scant crowd and that's for sure," she moaned to Austin. "And some of my chief parts are taken by country kids."

Austin sympathized. "You'll just have to use readers for the parts," he suggested. "Even adults could fill the gaps."

But it turned out that even the town folks were not able to make it to the program. The storm raged on. Austin made his way to the church and posted a notice on the door. "Christmas Program postponed until further notice," it stated simply, but Anna's heart was heavy. How would the children respond? They had worked so hard for the program. Surely they would be as disappointed as she herself.

They hoped that the program could be given on

Monday night, then changed to Tuesday night, then Christmas Eve. None of those worked. The weather held cold, with strong winds and drifting snow. At last, Anna accepted the inevitable. Christmas would come and go and their program would not be presented. She felt a deep sadness and disappointment as she resigned herself to the fact.

But the little town was not prepared to dismiss all the work and anticipation quite as easily.

"I think we should still have it," said Mrs. Brady the first Sunday of January.

"But Christmas is over," Anna replied, downhearted.

"No matter. The weather kept most of us from feeling like we really celebrated Christmas. No reason we can't go ahead and have it now."

Others voiced or nodded agreement. The idea was presented to Austin.

"If you feel there is still interest, I see no problem with that," he agreed. "I know that Anna and the children have put hours and hours of work into their program."

And so it was arranged. New posters were tacked in conspicuous places. Anna had Austin set up the stage again. The costumes were pulled back out of storage, and children polished up their parts. Anna felt more nervous than ever.

But when the program was finally presented on January fifteenth, it was to a full house. No one seemed to mind that the Christmas season had passed. The story of the first Christmas was just as pertinent, just as meaningful, just as full of hope and promise as it would have been were it presented at the usual time.

"Now I feel that I've had Christmas," Anna heard one woman say to another as they left the church. Neither of the women were from the little congregation.

"Folks seemed to really enjoy the program," Austin said later. "It was a great idea. And who knows, it may have caused more reflection—more impact—coming after the season than it would have had it been at the appointed time."

Anna nodded dumbly. She was still shaking from her bout of nerves.

"And we certainly got a number of folks I've never seen in church before," Austin commented.

Anna had hardly noticed the crowd. She had been far too busy trying to keep her little troop cued for their performance.

"I've been thinking," went on Austin. "It might be a good idea to have an Easter program . . . much the same."

He said the words as if it were such a simple, reasonable thing to do. Anna looked at him with wide eyes.

"What do you think?"

Anna swallowed. Then nodded dumbly. If it would help the church and their ministry to the community, how could she say no?

But Austin quickly added, "Not this year. You'll be too busy with the new baby, but we might think about it for next year."

In spite of herself, Anna breathed a little sigh of relief.

⋎   ⋎   ⋎

"We are going to have another new parishioner," Austin announced one day, a strange smile playing about his lips.

Anna looked up from kneading bread.

"A fellow by the name of Burton Bloom stopped by the church. He's the young bachelor school-teacher from that little country school just west of town. We stopped by his place once when we were calling but found no one home. Remember?"

Anna had a faint recollection.

"The next time I called alone and was told that he'd 'think about it.' Well, he's been thinking for quite a spell, but it seems that he now has a bit more to think about."

Anna waited.

"He says he'll be in church on Sunday. Wanted to know the hour of meeting."

Austin smiled again.

"Then he asked a few—shall we say—rather revealing questions. I have a strong feeling that his sudden desire to attend the House of God has something to do with a certain young widow."

Anna stopped working the dough and looked at her husband.

"Well, all I can say," went on Austin with a grin, "is that maybe he is the answer to prayer. Mine. Yours. And a certain widow's."

And with that simple statement, Austin grinned again and left Anna to her bread baking and to ponder the fact that her "naive young husband" was possibly rather perceptive.

Chapter Seventeen

Passing Days

Anna's days were more than full. She spent as much time as she could with Mrs. Lawes. It was difficult because of the distance, but Anna went to the farm at least once each week.

With the passing weeks, Anna's coming child made everything she did just a bit more difficult. In fact, Anna's time of confinement was drawing near and Austin's concern kept her closer to home.

She had managed to fix a layette of sorts, but it was difficult. "We have two bed sheets," she had reasoned. "We can do with one. The comforter has a soft lining." So Anna cut up one of their sheets to make diapers. But even the sheet didn't yield many diapers—and Anna knew she was destined to spend much of her time over the laundry tub after the baby had joined them.

She went through her own closet and found a slip that would do just fine for baby things and sewed three little garments from the material. She saved pennies until she had enough for yarn, and knitted a sweater, bonnet, and booties. And then came a parcel from home. Anna lifted the soft material from the bundle, knowing that her mama had sacrificed to make it possible. "Egg money," she murmured to herself, wiping tears and thanking God for her mama's hens.

Two days later another parcel came. This one was from Austin's mother. The garments were more expensive. A little gown, two little shirts, and a pair of tiny shoes. Anna wept again.

And then a most delightful thing happened. The congregation—and community—gave Anna a baby shower. She looked around the circle of ladies, many who did not come to their church, a few that she hadn't yet met, and she was so overcome by gratitude that she could hardly swallow her egg-salad sandwich. Why had she fussed and worried? God was looking after her little one all the time.

❧   ❧   ❧

Margaret Mae arrived a few minutes after midnight on March eighth. She was robust and healthy and another miracle in Anna's eyes. Never had she been so overcome with emotion as she was when she held the precious baby in her arms for the first time.

"Isn't she beautiful?" she whispered to Austin, and he assured her that she certainly was.

"I think she will have your big eyes," he said, beaming, and Anna looked up in surprise. He said it as if it was an asset. Anna had always felt her eyes too big for her skinny little face.

Oh, I do hope not, she wanted to say, but she held her tongue.

Mrs. Paxton was the first to call. Anna heard the cane come thumping down the walk and was braced for the pounding on the door. But it did not come.

Instead, there was a soft "Yoo-hoo," and Anna chuckled as she called out for her visitor to come in.

The elderly woman entered, hobbling her way across the floor.

"Hear you got a girl," she remarked.

Anna nodded. She had just nursed the baby, who slept contentedly beside her.

"She's a little mite," said the woman, gruffness tainting her voice.

Anna had long since become used to it. She smiled, knowing it to be a cover-up. A habit developed over years of grousing.

"She'll grow," she said softly.

The woman nodded.

"What're you calling her?"

"We've named her Margaret Mae, but we will be calling her Maggie."

The elderly woman nodded again and thumped her cane on the wooden floor. *Another of her habits,* thought Anna.

The thumping stopped and Mrs. Paxton lifted her head.

"You okay?" she surprised Anna by asking.

"I'm fine," responded Anna cheerily.

"You look paler than your sheet," said the woman frankly.

"I feel fine. My color will return once the doctor lets me out of bed."

The woman nodded again. "You'd be smart not to rush it," she informed Anna bruskly. Then added, "You want some tea?"

"My husband was just home and fixed me some," Anna answered, then had second thoughts. "But another cup would be nice if you don't mind fixing us both one."

Mrs. Paxton had never taken tea with her before.

As the old woman rummaged around in her kitchen, Anna lifted herself to a sitting position and plumped her pillows.

Mrs. Paxton was soon back with a cup of tea in her hand.

"You take milk or sugar?" she asked.

Anna shook her head. She had long since given up both—out of necessity. "No," she said now. "It's fine—black."

Anna accepted the tea. "Do you have one for yourself?" she asked.

"I can only carry one at a time," she replied dourly. "This here leg of mine takes a hand, too." She shook her cane as she spoke, and Anna nodded.

The thump, thump of the cane went back to the kitchen, then returned to the bedroom. Anna indicated the one chair that crowded into the corner. "Move that shirt of my husband's," she offered.

But the woman quickly responded, "Looks like it needs washing—guess I can sit on it." And she did.

❧　　❧　　❧

As soon as Anna was back on her feet, she asked Austin to drive her out to the Lawes.

"Isn't it a bit early for you to be traveling?" he worried.

"I must see how Mandy's doing," Anna responded, feeling sorry about leaving the woman on her own for so long.

Austin finally conceded. But he drove the mare extra carefully.

Mandy Lawes seemed very glad to see Anna. She beamed her pleasure, then suddenly drew back. Her face turned pale, but she still held her smile and motioned Anna with her small bundle into her kitchen.

"I've meant to come to see your new baby ever since I heard about her birth," she said, and then added softly, "but I just couldn't bring myself to do it. I—I wasn't sure how—I mean—what—my feelings would be. About a baby."

"I understand," said Anna, wishing she had given the trip more thought.

There was a moment of awkward silence.

"Would you—would you like me to just—go?" she asked candidly.

"No. No. I must face it—sometime. It might as well be now," Mandy Lawes said bravely, then surprised Anna by adding, "Here—let me hold her."

Anna put small Maggie in the arms of the mother who was still grieving the loss of her own child and watched helplessly as the tears flowed down the young woman's cheeks.

This is a terrible mistake, Anna told herself. *A— a knowledgeable person—Mrs. Angus—would have never made such a blunder.*

"I'm so sorry," she tried to say and went to take her daughter back.

"No. No," said Mandy, clinging to the baby. "I— I need to cry. Just—please—just let me be for a few minutes."

Anna turned and left the kitchen.

Austin was just coming up the walk after tethering the mare. His eyes raised to Anna's in question and she dipped her head, feeling shamed by her error in judgment.

"Isn't she home?" Austin asked her.

Anna nodded her head, tears tracing little streams down her cheeks. She lifted a hand to wipe them away.

"What is it?" he asked, reaching out to take her hand.

"She—she asked me to leave her a moment—with—with Maggie. Oh, Austin, she is in there crying her heart out. I never should have come. I should have thought. The pain is still too fresh—too deep—for her to look at another baby."

Anna buried her face against her husband's shoulder and shook with her sobs.

He let her cry, patting her shoulder, squeezing her arm. When she was finished, she stepped back and looked up at him.

"I'm so sorry. I suppose they'll never come to church now. It's all my fault."

"Nonsense," said Austin, offering his handkerchief. "If they don't come to church, it has nothing to do with this. You've offered your love and friendship over and over, in every way you have known how."

He waited for her to wipe her nose.

"One never knows how a person will respond in grief—or what will bring healing. Perhaps baby Maggie is a better counselor than either of us could ever be."

Anna looked up at him, her eyes wide.

"Holding that little bundle might be the best thing that could happen to Mrs. Lawes," went on Austin. "There are more than one kind of tears. Let's pray these are tears of healing."

They bowed their heads, standing together on the front walk, their hearts and hands twined closely. They had just said their "Amens" and Anna given her nose one more blow when they heard the door behind them open.

Mandy Lawes was still clutching tightly to Maggie, but the tears had been wiped away.

"I'm sorry," she said, her lips still trembling. "Please come in. I—I think that I am ready for company now."

🌿   🌿   🌿

The Lawes joined the little congregation the next Sunday.

"We have put it off for far too long," said Cal. "These kids need some religious training." And then he added, almost under his breath, "And we need some faith to live by."

🌿   🌿   🌿

One of the nice "extras" the new church offered was that they were able to make Austin an office in a small back room, and Anna was able to have her whole sitting room as living area. They needed the extra space. It was the only place that they could fit a small bed for Maggie.

Anna couldn't believe how quickly the baby grew. She was hard put to keep her in little garments. But each time the new mother was about to be smothered by desperation, there was another little miracle—and Maggie was clothed.

Washings, though, were not easy for Anna. With so few clothes for the baby, she had to wash almost every day of the week. She kept a tub of water on hand behind the kitchen stove and washed diaper by diaper as they were used. Then she hung them on the line and prayed that one of them would be dry by the time she needed it.

It was a difficult way to do her laundry, but Anna did not complain. She was thankful to have diapers at all.

But her hands became red and her knuckles rough from her scrub board.

I wish I had some lard to rub into them, she often thought and was glad she had gloves to wear on Sundays.

Chapter Eighteen

Another Summer

When the noise from the play lot picked up in volume, Anna felt that summer had really arrived. Once school was out the children had more free time so made good use of the play area. Anna sometimes stood at her bedroom window and watched the sand-lot ball game.

It was about a week into July before she realized that Ben Cross was missing. It was strange. Ben loved playing ball.

She picked up young Maggie and made her way out to the playground.

As soon as there was a break in the action, she motioned Tommy over.

"Where is Ben?" she asked the boy.

"He's sick," answered Tommy and was about to run back out on the field.

"How sick?" called Anna.

Tommy turned and flung back over his shoulder, "Don't know. Haven't seen 'im."

Anna scanned the field for Sid, Ben's younger brother. He was playing right field.

I'll just wait and ask him, she thought and found a place to sit on a patch of grass.

We should have checked on them, she scolded

herself. *Neither of them has been to Sunday school for several Sundays.*

But the boys' attendance had always been sporadic at best. How would one guess that illness might be keeping them at home?

When Sid came near to wait for his turn at bat, Anna called to him and he hastened to answer her bidding.

"I hear your brother Ben is sick," said Anna.

He nodded, his tangled hair bouncing.

"How long has he been ill?" she pressed him.

"Long time," he said with a shrug.

"What's the matter?"

"We don't know."

"Has the doctor seen him?"

Sid shook his head. "Pa don't put no stock in doctors," he replied and Anna cringed.

"Can you tell me a little bit about his illness?" asked Anna.

Sid looked blank. "He's just sick," he answered.

"Sick how? Does he have a rash? Is he vomiting? Does he have a fever?"

Sid seemed to be thinking about it. "He don't got a rash," he answered. "An' I don't think he vomits. He just throws up and can't eat."

Anna nodded, a smile curving her lips in spite of her concern.

It was Sid's turn to bat. Anna let the boy go. She hoisted Maggie onto her hip and started back to her kitchen.

Once there she deposited the baby on the floor and began searching through her cupboards. There wasn't much there. Maybe enough for a nourishing eggnog. She went to work.

As soon as she had prepared the drink, she put her bonnet in place, tied a hat on small Maggie, and set out.

It didn't take long to reach the Crosses. Anna had never been there before. She worried about the dog as she neared the place. The animal had a reputation for meanness. Perhaps she should have left the baby with her father at the church study. But Mr. Cross was seated on the rickety porch and with one word from him, the growling dog lay back down.

"I heard that Ben is sick," Anna said before the man had a chance to ask her errand. The burly man just nodded. Anna's eyes took in the sullen face, the arms and shoulders muscled from heavy work, the large calloused hands.

Mr. Cross was known as the hardest worker in the town. He ran the local livery and cartage service—and drove his teams almost as hard as he drove himself. He was so busy "earning" and "squirreling it away" according to some that he had no time for friends or family. Anna marveled that she had found him on his front porch, seemingly doing nothing.

"I've brought Ben a bit of eggnog," she said simply. "Sid said that he has been having trouble eating."

The man nodded again.

"May I see him?" Anna asked.

"He's in there," the man nodded over his shoulder, and Anna accepted that as his permission.

She moved toward the door and was about to enter when she thought of her baby girl. What if the illness was contagious? Surely she should have left Maggie with her father. Now what could she do?

For one brief second she hesitated and then she surprised both herself and the man who sat before her. "Would you mind holding my baby?" she asked simply. "It might be wiser not to take her into the sickroom."

For a moment the man stared, his expression saying that no one had ever entrusted a baby to him before. Him with his work-dirtied hands and gruff manner. Him with his violent temper and foul mouth. What was she thinking of—passing the small child in her unrumpled, spotless dress to him?

Dumbly he reached out his hands to accept the baby.

"Thank you," said Anna with a sweet smile and moved through the door with her container of eggnog.

A woman rocked listlessly in a corner. Anna could hear the low groan of the floor as the rocker moved slowly back and forth. On a cot against the wall lay Ben. Anna could hardly recognize the boy. His face was flushed, his eyes hollow, and he looked as if he had lost several pounds.

"I heard that Ben is ill," Anna said to the woman in explanation.

The woman nodded. She looked fatigued.

"I've brought some eggnog," said Anna.

The woman's eyes showed surprise but she did not stir.

"Do you have a cup?" asked Anna.

Without a word the woman roused herself and went to the kitchen. She came back with a cup, wiping it on a tea towel as she came. Anna could read the words "Robin Hood" imprinted on the towel.

Anna accepted the cup and knelt beside the sick boy. "Ben," she coaxed him. "Ben. It's Mrs. Barker. Can you hear me, Ben?"

He stirred ever so slightly.

"I've brought you something to drink," went on Anna. "Can you try to swallow for me? Come on . . . just a little. Here, try a sip. Good boy. Another."

A tongue came out and licked the dry lips. Anna was encouraged. "Another," she coaxed. "That's good."

He wasn't able to finish the drink but Anna was pleased with his attempt. The mother who hovered near her elbow spoke for the first time. "That's the first he's taken in two days."

"I'll leave the rest," said Anna. "You can try to give him a bit later on."

The woman nodded.

"I'll try to get some eggs and milk so I can bring more later. If we can just get him to take some nourishment . . ." Anna let the statement trail off.

"Do you have a cloth and some cool water?" Anna continued, and the woman went back to her kitchen. A little later Anna heard the pump in the backyard.

It wasn't long until Mrs. Cross was back at Anna's side. "Here," she said as she passed Anna a piece of an old towel and a basin filled with the water.

Anna took the rag and dipped it in the water. It was fresh and cool. She began to bath the face and arms of the young boy.

"This will help to get his fever down," she explained to the woman. "You can do this every hour or so. It will help him to feel better, too."

The mother nodded. Anna was sure that she had previously given up.

Ben stirred as the cool cloth passed again and again over his fevered face.

"There you are, Ben," said Anna. "That should make you feel better," and Anna dipped the cloth into the basin once more just as she heard giggles from the front porch. Apparently the big man was entertaining young Maggie.

"You look tired," said Anna, turning her attention to the woman.

Mrs. Cross nodded. "It's been almost a week of little sleep," she admitted. "I'm almost done in."

"You should have asked for help," said Anna softly.

"We don't have any family here," replied the woman.

"Well, neighbors would have—"

"We're not on friendly terms with the neighbors," cut in the woman.

"My husband or I will come tonight," offered Anna, "so you folks can get a good sleep."

Surprise showed in the woman's eyes. After a moment's silence, she spoke. "You're thet preacher's wife, aren't you?"

Anna nodded. "We have been so happy to have your boys come to Sunday school now and then."

"They sneaked out to do it," the woman replied, her voice dropping to a whisper. "We just figured they was off to play at first—then the truth came out. My man gave 'em a good thrashing when he found out."

Anna cringed. How cruel to treat young children in such a fashion. Especially when they had done no wrong. They had simply gone to Sunday school. And then she trembled. The child beater was holding her baby.

She rose to her feet and turned to the door just as she heard young Maggie squeal and giggle again.

"I must get home now." She hesitated for one moment. "But I'll be back," she said. Her thoughts went further, *And I'll leave my baby with her father,* but she did not say the words.

But the scene on the front porch stopped her mid-stride. There was the big man, a satisfied grin on his bearded face, Maggie balanced carefully on one knee, while his free hand tossed a worn-out sock that the brute of a dog was racing to retrieve. And young Maggie's arms were flailing, her eyes sparkling as she enthusiastically enjoyed the sport.

Anna smiled and stepped out of the darkened room. She did not move to claim her daughter immediately. Instead, she leaned against a porch pillar, letting her eyes lift to the livery stables where horses milled in a fenced yard. Anna wondered if they had been fed. Mr. Cross was known to take better care of his teams than of his boys. They were his "bread and butter," he said candidly.

"Your son is very sick, isn't he?" Anna commented with sympathy.

The man shuffled little Maggie a bit closer in his lap but made no reply.

"I know how worried I would be if it were my child," Anna went on.

She turned slightly to look at the man holding her baby. Maggie was reaching up a chubby hand to try to grasp a handful of beard.

"He did drink the eggnog," Anna said encouragingly. "I'll bring him more later. If he can just keep it down—"

She stopped her comment.

The big dog approached the man and nuzzled his nose up against Maggie, who squealed with delight.

So much for big bad dog, thought Anna, and smiled to herself.

"I had heard he was vicious," she said in good humor, indicating the dog who was allowing Maggie to pull his hair.

"He can rip the leg off a mule," replied the man matter-of-factly.

"Then why—?" began Anna.

The man shrugged. "Takes a pretty mean brute to resist a baby," he admitted, and his voice was low and trembling.

Anna stood without comment, blinking away tears that threatened to come. At last she straightened and moved toward the man and her child. She heard a growl deep in the throat of the dog, and the man spoke to him firmly.

"Doesn't realize she's yours," he apologized. "Already laid his claim on her."

"If I ever need a guard dog," said Anna as she reached for Maggie, "I'll know where to find him."

The big man couldn't hide a bit of a grin.

❧   ❧   ❧

Anna continued to take eggnog, then soup and stew to the young boy. And Austin took his turn several nights staying with the Crosses so the family could get some sleep. The condition of the young boy slowly but gradually improved. And at last the day came when Ben was able to sit up on his own again.

From then on he seemed to gain ground rapidly.

"Before you know it, you'll be out playing ball," Austin teased one day as he and Anna stopped to see Ben.

The boy grinned.

Mrs. Cross came from the kitchen with a pitcher of lemonade. "First place he's gonna go is to church," she said with feeling.

Austin and Anna exchanged brief glances. This was an unexpected change. Neither dared to make comment. Anna stole a quick glance in the direction of Mr. Cross to try to read his reaction.

He was bouncing Maggie on his big knee. From the beginning he had claimed her as "his girl," and she seemed to agree, grinning and clapping whenever they met.

"Was a time I wouldn't allow my boys to go to church," he admitted without looking up.

"Now you will?" prompted Austin.

The big head came up and the man looked directly at the town minister. "Not without me," he said simply.

᯽   ᯽   ᯽

No one in the whole town would have guessed that Matt Cross would be the preacher's first convert. Anna's prayers had zeroed in on the gruff Mrs. Paxton and the Lawes family. Even on the hard-to-read Mr. Parks, who kept helping God with His little miracles, though he refused to darken the church door.

It was true that Mrs. Paxton had softened over the months, but she still spoke gruffly, still scowled at the world, and still refused to attend services.

"I gave you my building," she said tartly, "but I didn't say that I came with it."

Anna knew better than to press the issue. She continued to offer her time and friendship.

The Lawes family were faithful in their attendance, but when Austin asked them if they wished to make a personal commitment to the faith, they stalled.

"It isn't that we are unbelievers," argued Cal; "we just aren't ready to take that step yet. I guess we're both still hurting. Need time to heal. Still feelin' a bit numb inside."

So Austin and Anna had waited and prayed, wondering just who would be the first to break the months of "drought" in their ministry.

But never, never had either of them supposed that it might be the misfit at the edge of town.

"God works in mysterious ways," Anna quoted after the big man had knelt at the little church altar rail and sobbed as he asked the Lord to forgive his sin and cleanse his heart.

It was an occasion for great rejoicing.

The man had been known in the community for so long as a work-driven, money-grubbing individual. Because of his drive, he'd had time for no one. His only distraction seemed to be whiskey. He would be sober and hard working for months on end, then suddenly lay aside his self-assigned tasks and pick up a bottle. When he drank he was an entirely different man. His family tried to stay well out of his way, his wife suffering the most from his abuse. Even his vicious dog was afraid of him.

And now the man had made the commitment of his life. He had become the first convert in the little village church.

The next logical event, in Anna's thinking, was for Mrs. Cross to join her husband in his commitment. But though Austin spoke to the woman and explained carefully how one accepted the wonderful gift of God's forgiveness, she held back. She wanted her boys taught "religion." She didn't begrudge her husband his step of faith. But she would just wait and see.

Anna was understanding. "She has lived with an angry, abusive man for so many years that I'm sure it must be hard for her to believe even the Lord can change him," she said to Austin. "We'll just have to allow her time for observation."

Austin nodded, but both of them knew it was difficult to wait when a person's soul was at stake.

Chapter Nineteen

Baptism

Anna's days seemed to be more than full, what with the garden, calling, housekeeping, care of baby Maggie, and duties at the church.

She still lamented her lack of leadership. She felt there was so much more that could be accomplished in their little congregation if only Austin had a better qualified partner for his work. But it was a joy to watch Mr. Cross grow in his faith. Besides attending the Sunday services, he was meeting once a week with Austin, where together they studied the Scriptures about the Christian life.

Young Ben gained strength steadily and finally joined his shouts to the racket from the baseball diamond on the lot across the back alley. Anna shivered when she thought of how close they had been to losing him.

The summer was dry and farmers fretted about the hay crop. "Hardly enough there to make it worth one's while," Anna heard again and again.

"Well, it's all we'll get," said another. "We'll have to take what we can."

But there was uneasiness. Folks feared there wouldn't be enough feed to get their animals through the winter.

In spite of the dry year, Anna was pleased with her garden. She had spent some of the hot summer days hauling up pails of water from the nearby creek, but it had been worth the effort. Anna was thankful for a good return. One that she counted on to get them through another winter. The final task of gathering was all that remained to be done.

჻ ჻ ჻

" 'Fraid I have some bad news," said Mrs. Landers one Sunday morning when she met Anna at the door of the little church.

Anna's eyes opened wide. She did hope no one else was sick.

"Neighbor's pigs got out," Mrs. Landers explained.

Anna found herself wondering what that had to do with her.

"Never touched my garden—but they most ruined yours," went on the woman.

Anna felt her heart sink. What would they ever do without a garden?

She found it difficult to concentrate on Austin's sermon, and when Maggie began to fuss, Anna used it as an excuse to get out to some fresh air. She felt she was suffocating.

Surely it isn't that bad, she tried to tell herself. *I've seen gardens rooted by pigs. It always looks as though they have taken everything—but they leave a lot behind.*

It wouldn't do to walk out to the garden on the Lord's Day. Anna had to hold herself in check, but it was an awful long wait until the next morning.

"The pigs have been in my garden," she told Austin. "I'm going out to check the damage."

The sun was still hanging in the eastern horizon and the water for the morning's washing was boiling on the back of the kitchen stove. Austin knew that Anna's concern must be great.

"Would you like me to go see?" he asked.

"No, I need to see for myself," responded Anna.

"Do you want me to come with you?"

"No. But if I could leave Maggie? She's still sleeping."

He nodded and Anna slipped on her work bonnet and set out at a brisk pace.

It was worse than she would have dared to think. Almost all her precious garden was taken. Here and there a half eaten potato still lay on the ground. Scattered down the long rows were a few missed carrots, a turnip or two. But for all intents and purposes, the whole summer's work was gone.

Anna could have cried, but instead she set herself to picking up the few remaining vegetables.

"God," she prayed as she worked. "You know all about this. You know how much we thought we needed this garden. I know that you have promised to supply our needs, so I guess you have other plans, Lord. Help me to be patient as I wait to see what they are."

Anna had about gathered the last of the scattered pieces of vegetables when she heard a team on the road. The driver pulled the horses to a stop and climbed down heavily. She recognized the man as Mr. Briggs, the local attorney.

"Heard you had your garden raided," he said as he walked toward her.

Anna nodded solemnly.

"That man has never kept his hogs fenced properly. Been a problem over and over. Folks are getting mighty sick of his slackness."

Anna said nothing.

"I'm sure folks will side in with you if you lodge a formal complaint," he instructed. "Everyone knows that you needed those vegetables. You might not get all you have coming, but the court would at least make him stand good some of the damage."

Anna looked up in surprise, then managed a weak smile.

"No," she said softly. "Scripture says that we aren't to take a brother to court."

"He's not a brother," argued Mr. Briggs. "He hasn't been near a church since his mama had him christened."

Anna threw another piece of potato in her pail and sighed.

"The truth is, Mr. Briggs," she said slowly, "I have no idea how we'll ever make it through the winter ahead. But I wouldn't feel right about taking anyone to court. We'd never have a chance to win the man to the Lord if we did such a thing."

Mr. Briggs shrugged and kicked at a lump of dirt at his feet.

"And that is more important than eating?" asked the man, a bit sarcastically.

"Yes," said Anna, meeting his eyes directly and evenly. "Yes, it is."

The man shuffled uncomfortably for a minute, gazing off into the distance to avoid the candid eyes of the small woman. Anna reached to pick up one more chunk of carrot.

"Whose pigs are they, anyway?" she asked, and then wished she hadn't. It would have been easier not to carry a grudge if she didn't know.

"Fella by the name of Carl."

Carl? thought Anna. The name was familiar. And then she remembered the young boy. Carl. She hadn't seen him for some time. She had liked the shy lad. Well, that was one more reason for not pressing for damages.

"We'll manage," said Anna with more confidence than she felt. "I'm not sure how—but God won't let us down."

Mr. Briggs nodded, but it was clear that Anna was beyond his understanding. He wished her a good day and left her alone.

Anna was just about to pick up her pails of vegetables and head for home when Austin arrived carrying Maggie.

He surveyed the damage and reached out his hand to Anna. "Pretty bad, eh?" he commented.

Anna nodded. There was no use denying it.

"Too late to plant anything," observed Austin, and again Anna nodded. Though the weather was still nice, it was time for harvesting, not planting.

"That's all that was left?" asked Austin, nodding his head toward the pails.

"That's all," said Anna wearily.

Austin handed Anna the baby and picked up the pails.

"Guess we might as well get them on home," he said and they started off together.

205

Word soon spread. Carl's pigs had completely destroyed the preacher's crop, but the preacher had no intention of suing.

Some folks saw the decision as noble. Other folks thought the parson a fool. After all, he did need the vegetables and he certainly had a good case. The pigs had been caught in the act, and everyone knew where they came from.

Austin was completely unaware of the comments that swirled around them.

But when the talk finally settled down, the one fact remained. The local preacher was more interested in the soul of a man than he was in his own welfare. In spite of themselves, the community folks could not help but admire such a man.

No one seemed to know that it was Anna who had turned down the invitation to present a lawsuit.

❧   ❧   ❧

"Matt wants to be baptized," announced Austin, his voice filled with excitement. Anna shared his joy.

"That's wonderful!" she exclaimed.

Fall was upon them, with winter fast approaching. It really didn't seem to be a good time of year to be baptizing folks in the local stream.

"When?" was Anna's question.

"Just as soon as we can arrange it."

"This fall yet?"

Austin nodded. "I hope we can get it all in place for next Sunday. I need to meet with the board. They will want to hear his statement of faith."

It's too cold, Anna wanted to object, but she held her tongue. Austin was the one to make such decisions. He was the minister of the church.

The church board met with the candidate and expressed satisfaction with his responses and recommended him for baptism. The final arrangements were made.

They met at the creek for the morning service. The day was cold with a brisk wind blowing from the north. Anna felt herself fidgeting and scolded herself for her lack of faith.

It was a thrill to see Austin's first convert as he waded out into the stream and stood, tears running down his face as he witnessed to his new-found faith to all those who watched from the shore.

"I know I've had a reputation in this town," he told them. "A reputation that I'm not proud of. But God has changed all that. You are looking at a new man. A new Matt Cross. From now I hope to gain a *new* reputation. One of love and compassion toward my family and neighbors. One of devotion to my Lord. I have seen that kind of love and devotion in action. It opened my eyes to the truth."

He looked directly at Anna when he said the words.

Even in baptism he is looking at his little Maggie, thought Anna, who was holding her small daughter, and tears came to her eyes.

After the baptismal ceremony, Matt wrapped himself in a wool blanket and huddled together with his family.

Austin stood before the group in his wet clothes and preached a short sermon from the Word.

He'll catch his death of cold, Anna fretted. *The*

wind will chill him to the bone.

They had discussed the problem. He should have had a change of clothes. But he had only one Sunday suit.

"I will keep the message short," Austin had promised Anna, and she had to be satisfied with that.

But by the time they had traveled home in the buggy, Austin was so cold that his teeth were chattering.

"You get out of those wet clothes and into bed," Anna told him. "I'll take care of the mare."

He didn't argue. Picking up Maggie, he hurried into the house.

When Anna returned from the barn where the mare was stabled, he was still shivering. He had removed the wet clothes and pulled on some old pants and a heavy shirt, but the fire had died down and the room was cool.

Anna sent him to get a quilt off the bed while she busied herself with stirring up the fire again.

Unconcerned, Maggie crawled about the room, investigating things that she had left behind that morning.

"You need some hot soup," Anna said to her husband, but she did not have hot soup. She fixed hot tea instead.

"Here drink this . . . then get to bed."

The dinner was a simple one. Steamed vegetables, a fried egg, and bread. Anna wished she had something more nourishing.

Austin continued to shiver for most of the day in spite of Anna's attempts to warm him. She heated towels in the oven and kept rotating them in his bed, tucking them in closely around him. Still he shook.

He'll catch a death of cold, she fretted.

By nightfall he had stopped shaking. By morning he was flushed with fever. He coughed and sneezed by turn and Anna knew they were in for a good fight.

She needed something nourishing. She needed broth. But there was no meat in the house—and no hope of getting any. Anna fixed cups of tea and coaxed her husband to drink as much as he could.

By evening his cold was even worse. *If only I had chicken,* Anna thought. *I could make him chicken soup. Mama always made chicken soup to fight a cold.*

But Anna did not have chicken.

By the next day the cold had settled into his chest. Anna knew that she must keep him in bed. She made a mustard plaster and wrapped his throat with a wool sock dipped in kerosene.

That was all she could remember of her mother's secret remedies. Inwardly she fretted that she was no better at being a nurse than she was at being a minister's wife.

If only I had chicken, she fussed again. And then Anna took her need to the Lord in prayer.

"God, I don't know how to treat such a bad cold. The only thing I know is chicken soup—and I don't have a chicken. Show me what to do, Lord."

It was late in the afternoon when Anna decided to run to the store. Clutching a few coins in her hand and holding her shawl closely about her, she hurried down the walk to the street. Perhaps she had enough money for a drumstick or a thigh.

Maybe even a wing. She'd swallow her pride and see what Mr. Parks would do for her.

She had just pushed through the gate when she nearly ran into Mr. Brady.

In his hand he carried the biggest rooster Anna had ever seen. She slid to a stop and stared at the bird.

"Wagon wheel ran right over his neck," he said, reading the question in her eyes. "Missus said to get rid of him. She was in no mood to cook up this tough old bird."

Anna still stared, her eyes wide, mouth dropping open.

"I thought Mr. Parks might like him for his dog. Couldn't feed him to mine—might make a chicken killer of him—but Parks' dog isn't around chickens."

Anna swallowed hard and found her voice.

"When—when did it happen?" she asked shakily.

"Just happened. Figured the dog might prefer him while he's still warm."

Anna lifted her eyes from the dangling rooster. She decided to be honest and direct. Austin's health depended on nourishment.

"Mr. Brady," she said slowly. "I have just been praying for chicken to make soup for my husband. I—I—"

It was his turn to look surprised.

"You want this old fella?" he said, lifting up the bird.

"If—if you wouldn't mind," replied Anna.

"He'll be tough."

"I'll stew him."

For a moment he looked doubtful and then he slowly extended the rooster to Anna. "I rung his neck soon as I hit him," he said, "so he should be fine for eating."

Thank you, Lord, said Anna inwardly and reached out to accept the bird.

"Expect you might have to stew him for a long time," apologized Mr. Brady. "He's been around for a lot of years."

But Anna was not worrying. The Lord had answered another prayer.

"Thank you. Thank you," she was saying over and over, not sure in her own heart if she was talking to Mr. Brady or her God. She waved the hand that still clutched its coins and turned toward the house.

"Thought she was off to somewhere," she heard Mr. Brady say to himself as she hurried away. But she didn't stop to explain. She was anxious to get the big rooster into the stewing pot.

❧   ❧   ❧

Anna never did know if it was the chicken soup that started Austin on the mend or just the natural course of the illness. But she was always quite willing to give God all the credit for supplying the chicken at just the right time. The whole family had enjoyed the rich chicken soup.

Chapter Twenty

Disturbing News

Ben and Sid entered her kitchen when she answered their knock. It was not unusual for them to pay her a visit. They would run in occasionally to see Maggie, share some exciting bit of news, or look longingly toward her bread crock.

Anna sensed that something was different about this visit. The boys did not rush to play with Maggie. They did not begin on some adventure story, with both trying to tell her about it at once as they usually did. They did not even glance toward her bread crock. They took chairs by her table and sat silently, shuffling their feet and fiddling with their hands.

Anna tried to draw them out, but their answers were short and to the point, with no excitement coloring the words.

"Ball season over?"

"A-huh."

"Are you enjoying school?"

"Kinda."

"What grade are you in?"

"Five." "Four." Both words spoken at the same time.

"How's your mother?"

"Okay." But Anna noticed shifting of position and an uneasiness in eyes when they answered. Something was wrong.

"Your mother isn't sick, is she?" she asked quickly.

"No."

Anna went for a loaf of bread and her small jar of home-made rhubarb marmalade.

"Is something wrong at your house?" she asked as she sliced bread, not even lifting her head to look at either of them.

There was no answer. Anna looked up.

"Is there?" she asked again, looking directly at Ben.

"Uncle Mort's there," he answered as though that should explain things.

"Who's Uncle Mort?" asked Anna, but she felt an uneasiness stealing through her.

"Pa's brother," said Sid.

"Is he just visiting?" asked Anna.

Troubled eyes looked up at her. "Sometimes he stays," answered Ben.

Anna let the matter drop while she handed out the bread slices. Something was wrong. But she had no idea what it was.

The boys ate their bread and marmalade and then left the house. Anna heard their shouts later from over at the local playground. They had found some other fellows for a game of tag.

"I wonder what's going on?" Anna said to young Maggie. "Maybe you and I should just take a walk." And so saying, Anna got her hat and shawl and a bonnet and coat for her daughter and left for the Crosses.

As soon as she entered the yard she knew that something was indeed wrong. The place had a different feel—a different look—a different smell.

The big mutt of a dog was no problem. He knew them well enough to welcome them with a wag of his stubby tail. Maggie wanted to stop and pet him but Anna kept heading toward the house.

She knocked on the door but there was no response. She rapped more loudly and waited again. Still nothing. She was about to turn and leave when she heard a voice behind her. It startled her and she jumped, turning around quickly at the sound.

"Won't get any answer from that pair." It was Mrs. Cross.

"Oh," said Anna, her hand fluttering near her face. "I wasn't expecting you from that direction."

Mrs. Cross just nodded.

"Is—is anything wrong?" Anna dared to ask.

"Mort is here," said Mrs. Cross.

There it was again. An answer that wasn't an answer.

"Yes—the boys told me—but—"

Mrs. Cross sighed deeply and crossed to the old rocker on the porch and slowly lowered herself. She looked tired—pained. Anna couldn't understand it.

"Go on in and see for yourself," the older woman said with a nod of her head.

Anna stared at the woman.

"Here," the woman continued, holding out her arms toward Maggie. "Leave the youngster with me."

Maggie was placed in the outstretched arms and Anna steeled herself before opening the door.

The room was a shambles. Anna wasn't sure if

215

its occupants had been fighting or celebrating. Everything seemed to be scattered across the floor, including items that should have still been on bodies.

Shirts, shoes, and socks were among the other debris. And then Anna noticed the bottles. That was the smell. Liquor. Anna raised her eyes to the form slumped in the corner. It was a man. Mort must—

But to Anna's horror her eyes rested instead upon Matt Cross.

For one instant she feared that he must be ill— maybe even dead. She crossed to him, almost tripping over another body. The man on the floor was big, bearded, and bloated. But he looked like Matt. Mort? He was sprawled across the floor as if someone had downed him. Had there been a battle?

A groan from the corner told Anna that at least Matt was still alive. She hurried on to him.

"Oh, I wish I had stopped for Austin," she said aloud. "I have no idea—"

But when she bent over the man, it was not so hard to tell the cause of his condition. Matt Cross was dead drunk.

Anna felt ill with grief and disappointment. All *that* was to have been behind him. He had been forgiven his life of sin. He had been baptized. He was a member of the local church. How could he? How could he ever do such a thing?"

She wanted to weep. She wanted to protest. And then to Anna's surprise she realized that she wanted to reach out and smack the man smartly, right across his puffed, whiskered face.

But she did none of those things. She bowed her

head and a moan escaped her lips. "Oh, God," she prayed. "What has he done? This shouldn't have happened. *This shouldn't have happened.* His testimony. Everyone in the town has been watching him. His wife— She will never be won now. Oh, God."

And Anna put her face in her hands and wept. The accuser began to thrust darts at her soul. "It was your fault" came the evil whisper. "You thought that just because he had prayed for salvation, he would never be tempted again. You let him down. You haven't been calling—encouraging like you should have been. You let the whole church down. You've ruined your husband's reputation in this town. His religion doesn't work, folks'll say. There's the proof. It doesn't work. Austin's first convert. A failure. No one will listen now. You might as well quit."

Quit—quit—quit. The word seemed to echo back and forth in Anna's head.

Suddenly her back straightened and resolve filled her eyes.

"We can't quit," she said as though speaking to someone in the room. "I might have failed—but I won't quit," and she braced her shoulders and headed for the kitchen. She had heard that strong coffee helped to sober people in Matt Cross's condition.

By the time Anna had the coffee ready, she could hear groanings from the other room. She didn't know if it was Matt or his brother Mort who was making the noises. Maybe both. She didn't go to check. She didn't even want to look at them. She wished she never had to look at the scene again.

But she needed help. She knew so little about drunkenness.

She went out the back door and around to the front of the house where Mrs. Cross still sat, idly entertaining Maggie.

"Would you go to the church office and ask Pastor Barker to come, please?" she asked and was surprised at the calmness in her voice.

The woman arose without a word and lifted young Maggie up into her arms. She had taken a few steps before she turned and looked at Anna.

"They won't wake up for hours yet," she said from experience. "But when they do—you don't want to be here."

And she turned again and went on down the dusty path.

Anna puzzled over the statement as she went back around the house and into the kitchen.

❦   ❦   ❦

Austin's initial response was much like Anna's. "How could he? How could he?" he kept repeating over and over as he bent over the two inert bodies.

"It's the drink," said Mrs. Cross with resignation. "Once it gets hold of a man, ain't nothing that can break him loose."

Anna wished to argue but it didn't seem like the right time. Their hope of proving to Mrs. Cross that her husband was a changed man seemed to have slipped away. They would never convince her now.

"No use wasting coffee," said the woman. "They'll wake up when they wake up. An' when they do—they'll wake up swingin'."

"You'd better go home," Austin said to Anna. "I'll wait here with Mrs. Cross."

Anna looked from her husband to her small baby. She hated to leave Austin, but if things were to get as ugly as Mrs. Cross seemed to think they would, she did not want little Maggie endangered. She nodded dumbly and was about to pick up her little girl.

But Mrs. Cross was moving toward the cupboards. "Both of you better go," she said, her voice sounding flat but firm. "I've been through it before. I know what to expect. No use taking chances on someone else getting hurt."

She lifted cups from the shelf and began to pour coffee. "As long as you made it, ain't no use wastin' this coffee," she said as she set the cups before them, picked up one for herself, and lowered her frame wearily into a chair at the kitchen table.

❦　　❦　　❦

They both went home. Heavy-hearted. Downcast. Disappointed. Grieved. It was difficult to even talk about their feelings. Their doubts.

Anna was putting supper on the table when she heard footsteps running down their walk. She went to the door even before there was a knock. Somehow she knew that it would be Ben and Sid.

"Ma says, can you come?" blurted out Sid.

"Pa's awake," added Ben, his eyes wide.

"Oh, dear God," prayed Anna and cast a glance toward Austin, who was giving Maggie a ride on his foot.

Anna looked from the table to Maggie.

"We'll feed her," offered Ben. "We'll look after her."

"Have you had your supper?" asked Anna as she laid aside her apron.

Both boys shook their heads.

"Then you go ahead and eat too," Anna offered. "Maggie's dish is there. Just give her vegetables. Mash them well."

They left together. It was hard not to run through the town, but Austin held their pace to a fast walk.

They had no idea what to expect when they got to the Crosses. As they neared the door, Austin's hand reached out to Anna's arm.

"You'd better wait here while I check it out," he warned, and Anna obeyed, though she would have preferred staying by the side of her husband.

It was quiet. Anna strained to hear sounds. What had happened? Was everyone in the house?

Old Mutt pushed himself up against her skirts and licked at her hand. Anna let her fingers trail over his shaggy head and massaged a loped ear.

Then she heard it. A low moaning. No, a sobbing. Someone was crying. What was happening in the eerie house? Anna moved forward just as the screen door opened and Austin looked out.

"Come in," he invited.

The room looked even worse than it had when she had seen it last. Anna was sure that a fight must have taken place.

The loud sobs were coming from the kitchen. Anna followed Austin, her throat so tight she could hardly breathe.

In a chair, slumped forward with his face in his

hands, sat Matt Cross. His shoulders were shaking with the sobs that shook his whole body. Anna had never heard such a terrible sound in all her life. The groans seemed to come from his very soul, to rend him bare with every rasping breath. She stood where she was, unable to move farther.

Mrs. Cross was dipping a cloth in a basin of water and wiping the man's head. It was then that Anna saw the blood. He seemed to have an ugly gash on the back of his head. Was it that painful, to cause such weeping?

"Where is Mort?" she heard Austin asking.

"He sent him away," Mrs. Cross answered without even looking up.

"Is he badly hurt?" Austin asked next.

"No—nothing serious. He's been hurt worse before."

"What can I—?" began Austin, crossing to the woman.

"Nothing now. I shouldn't have sent for you. I was scared. They was havin' a row. I was afraid that someone might get hurt—*really* hurt. I'm sorry. I shouldn't have—"

But Austin was reaching for the cloth, ready to take over the cleaning up of the wound.

"It's just that it never happened like that before. Where they turned on each other," the woman went on to explain.

Anna moved forward. She could hardly hear the words of the woman over the sobs of the man.

"They started rousing 'bout the same time," Mrs. Cross went on. "Mort started cussing and yelling and telling me to get some coffee—something to eat. So I started fixin' supper—but it wasn't fast enough for him. He threw a chunk of firewood at me. He missed, so weren't no harm done, but Matt took offense.

" 'Don't harm my missus,' he says and Mort cussed at him.

" 'You think you're the only one with the pleasure?' he says to Matt.

" 'Nobody has thet pleasure,' says Matt.

" 'What's the matter with you—you turned to mush?' says Mort. 'First you don't want to share my bottle—and now you're lily-livered 'bout the woman. You a man—or what?'

" 'I think you better leave my house,' says Matt.

" 'S'ppose a yellow-belly like you is gonna make me?' says Mort, and he started to swear something awful.

" 'If I have to, I will,' says Matt.

"That's when the fight broke out. I told the boys to get on out of there. I didn't know what might happen. These two had never turned on each other before. I was afraid someone might get badly hurt— or even killed. I didn't know what to do."

"You did the right thing," said Austin, still bathing the open wound.

"Maybe's he's hurt worse than I thought," said Mrs. Cross with concern. "I've never, ever heard him carry on like this before."

Austin knelt before the man. "Matt. Matt. What is it? Are you in pain? What's bothering—?"

But the man only sobbed harder.

"Maybe we should put him to bed," said Mrs. Cross, and Austin nodded. It looked as if the bleeding had stopped.

Anna stood by helplessly while Austin helped

Mrs. Cross get her husband to the bed in the next room. There seemed nothing to do but to go home. He was still crying when they left, but he appeared somewhat calmer.

"Well," said Anna as they walked home together, "this is about the biggest disappointment of my life. I thought . . . I mean, I really thought he had changed. That Mrs. Cross would see the change for herself and soon be—"

"So did I," agreed Austin, and his voice was equally pained. "He seemed so sincere."

They walked in silence for several minutes; then Anna asked softly, "What do we do now? The church will demand his membership be revoked."

She reached for Austin's hand.

"We'll have to discipline him. We have no choice," he answered.

Anna felt the tears sting her eyes. It was so heartbreaking. Their one and only convert. The one who had given their ministry new meaning—new purpose. And now it was lost. He was lost. "Oh, God," she prayed, "forgive us our failure. Our lack of wisdom and ability. We've let you down. I've let you down—again."

Chapter Twenty-one

Another Blow

"Mr. Parks was here," said Ben as soon as they had entered their kitchen.

"He wants to see you," added Sid, turning to face Austin.

Oh, dear, thought Anna, *has the word spread through the town already?*

Her eyes lifted to Austin's.

"Your mama wants you to come home now," Austin was saying to the two boys.

They moved toward the door without hesitation.

"Thank you for the supper," they both said as one and Anna nodded.

"And thank you for caring for Maggie," she replied with a smile.

The door closed and Maggie began to cry. Anna bent to pick her up and console her. "The boys will come again," she told the little girl. "Don't fuss. It's almost bedtime. No more time to play tonight. The boys will be back. Maybe tomorrow."

"I'd better go," said Austin.

"Don't you want to eat first?" Even as Anna asked the question, she knew that most of their supper had already been eaten.

"No. I'd better check. Mr. Parks isn't in the habit

of making social calls at the parsonage."

Anna could not help but smile, but a nervous twittering occurred somewhere deep inside. Why had Mr. Parks called and left word that he wanted to see Austin? She felt sure that he wasn't out to take part in another "miracle."

Austin left and Anna busied herself with getting Maggie prepared for bed.

She had just tucked the little girl in when she heard the door open. Austin was back. She gave Maggie one more kiss and returned to the kitchen.

Austin was pacing the floor, running his hand through his hair in his characteristic way.

"What is it?" asked Anna, fear gripping her.

"Mrs. Paxton," said Austin, turning to face her.

"Is she ill?"

"They found her in her bed. They judge that she has been dead for a couple of days."

"What?"

Austin nodded.

"But I just saw her—"

"Monday. That's the last anyone saw her. When she didn't come in for her weekly paper today, Mr. Parks got worried. They went to her house—and found her."

"I—I can't believe it!" cried Anna, the shock giving way to sorrow. She had learned to love the crusty old woman.

She eased herself into a kitchen chair. "Oh, Austin," she said as a new thought took her, "she hadn't made her peace with God."

Austin began to pace again. Anna could see the muscles of his jaw working.

Anna began to weep then.

Austin crossed to lift her so that he could hold her as she cried. "It's my fault. It's my fault," sobbed Anna.

"You couldn't have done anything further," Austin tried to comfort her. "She died in her sleep. No one could—"

"No!" cried Anna. "It's my fault she hadn't made her peace with God. I should have known something might happen. I should have—"

"Anna. Anna, hush," Austin scolded softly. "You did talk to her. Remember? She shook her cane at you and told you never to mention the subject again. You told me about it."

"But I didn't explain it like I should have. Mrs. Angus would have known what to say—how to say it. Any other minister's wife would have known. I— I stumbled and—and faltered and— Oh, Austin!"

Anna could go no further. She leaned her head against Austin's shoulder and wept for her friend and neighbor.

❧   ❧   ❧

They held the burial the next day. Mr. Parks was the one who made the arrangements.

"She left this sealed envelope with me, you see," he explained to Austin and Anna. "I wasn't to open it unless something happened. In it she said that she didn't want a funeral. Just a burial. No sermon or anything. She didn't put much stock in religion."

Austin nodded. He had to concede.

Anna wished to argue. *That was before,* she wished to say. *Before we came. Before she softened.*

*Before she gave us her building for a church.
Surely...*

But Anna, too, had to concede.

There were only a few neighbors at the cemetery
as the wooden casket was lowered. To Anna, it
seemed so strange—so awful, that no one was
speaking any word about the deceased. That no one
was asking God for His mercy—or even committing
the elderly woman's body to the ground. They all
just stood there and watched the coffin being lowered. Then they threw in a few handsful of dusty
soil and walked away. Anna had seen animals buried with more ceremony.

With a heavy heart she walked home through
the afternoon haze. It was all so sad. So final. Anna
felt she wouldn't be able to bear it. Mrs. Paxton was
gone—and she had failed her. Had failed her in the
worst possible way.

The church board met. Matt Cross had asked for
permission to appear before them. Anna's heart felt
heavy as she waited for Austin to come home from
the meeting.

At last she heard his step on the walk.

She rose to meet him, laying aside her Bible.
She had been reading and praying, but it was so
hard to concentrate.

Austin looked weary. Anna waited for him to
hang his hat on the peg.

"What happened?" she asked.

"He's been put on probation," he answered, knowing that was what she wanted to know.

"For how long?"

"Six months."

Anna turned and moved toward the stove. Her shoulders sagged. "Would you like some tea?" she asked.

He shook his head. "I think I'd like bed," he answered. "This week has been a month long."

Anna nodded. It had been a trying, a most discouraging, difficult week.

As they prepared for bed Austin spoke again.

"He was repentant. No excuses, only tears of sorrow. They didn't remove his membership—just asked him to prove himself before he would be granted full membership privileges."

Anna was glad to hear that.

"I guess it's easy to sit back and judge," went on Austin, "when you know nothing of the strong pull of drink. His brother brought along this bootleg liquor. At first Matt firmly refused, but Mort kept working on him. Told him how good it was—and just to take a little taste and see if it wasn't the best stuff he'd ever made.

"He took the first drink to try to get the guy off his back—but then there was no stopping."

For the first time since the incident, Anna felt a bit of compassion.

"It was a bad mistake," said Austin wearily, "but who isn't beyond making mistakes?"

But such a costly one, thought Anna. "He could have been a testimony to the entire town—and he failed" she said aloud. "He should have been an example to his wife of what faith could do, and he has messed that up too." It would take months, maybe years to gain back what he had lost. It was hard for Anna to forgive him.

"You should have seen him. He sobbed just like he did the night it happened."

Anna thought back to that night. The weeping of the man had left her with nightmares. She had never seen such sobbing.

"You mean—when he cried so—that night—it wasn't because he was hurt?"

"He was hurt—but that wasn't what brought the tears. He's a tough one. Mrs. Cross said she saw him walk on a broken leg without flinching."

"I thought maybe that was the way he acted when he came out of a—a drunk," admitted Anna, cringing at the crudeness of her own words.

"Guess some men do cry," acknowledged Austin, "but that wasn't his way. He usually was fighting mad. Crushing anything that he could get his hands on. Cursing and yelling and striking out. Everyone had to try to keep out of his way. Everyone."

"It's strange," mused Anna. "But if only he had stayed firm in his faith," she added.

"Well, that's behind us. No use dwelling on it. What counts now is what happens in the future. We had prayer together. God is willing to give him another chance—that's all that's really important."

Another chance, thought Anna. *That's what God is giving me. I need to pray more for the family. I need to show them I care. Really care.*

And then Anna's thoughts turned again to Mrs. Paxton. No possibility of another chance there. She had missed all opportunity to help the poor, bitter woman.

Oh, God, she mourned, *can you ever forgive me?*

☙   ☙   ☙

Anna followed through with her resolve. The very next day she went to call on the Crosses. She didn't know if the damage could ever be repaired, if Mrs. Cross would ever be convinced that Christianity was real, now that her husband had failed. But Anna decided that with God's help, she would do all she could.

The woman welcomed her readily enough and Anna was thankful for that. They sat on the porch together watching Maggie toss a rag for Mutt to retrieve. Anna had made up her mind that directness was the only way to approach the situation.

"We let your husband down," Anna admitted openly. "We should have supported him better. We didn't understand his temptation. We thought—well, we just thought that since he had asked for forgiveness—had accepted Christ—Christ can change hearts, you know—really—give an individual a new clean life—and heart. We thought that Matt would be changed. We—"

But the woman looked at Anna as though confused. "He *is* changed," she said firmly.

"But I mean—I mean changed from his—his former life."

"He is," defended the woman.

"But—" Anna began again, wondering why the woman couldn't understand her simple explanation.

"Mrs. Barker," said Mrs. Cross, leaning forward in her chair. "If you had known Matt, if you had seen him on a drunk, then you would know that he has changed."

"But—but he still—"

"Got drunk," finished the woman. "Yes. Yes, he did. But even under the influence of the liquor he was different. Don't you see? He was different. Even the drink did not change that. He drank until he passed out—but when he roused, he didn't come up cursing—screaming—throwing anything he put his hands on. No—he came up defending me— weeping like his heart would break in two for the remorse he felt. I've never seen him like that— never."

She stopped for a few moments, unable to go on. She wiped at her eyes with the hem of her green-checked apron and took a deep breath.

"Mrs. Barker," she said, looking directly at Anna, "right there beside his bed that night I knelt right down. I said, 'God, if you can change a man this much, then you are what I need. Change me, too, Lord. Change me, too.'"

With a glad cry Anna was out of her seat and kneeling beside the woman. They held each other, their tears tracing paths down smiling faces. Anna had no words to express her surprise—or joy.

⚜   ⚜   ⚜

In spite of the great rejoicing over the good news of Mrs. Cross, Anna walked through the days and weeks with heaviness. Austin sensed her change of spirit and tried to discuss it with her but Anna averted any prodding. She didn't know if her depression was because she was expecting their second child or because she was still grieving over the death of Mrs. Paxton. She had not realized just how attached she had become to the woman.

But Anna's burden was one far deeper than sorrow. It was guilt. Heavy guilt. Over and over she chastised herself for her clumsiness in her Christian witness. She prayed and she agonized, but she could not shake the heaviness that pulled her down.

She had failed—again. She, the wife of a minister. She had no business calling herself a partner in the faith. She was not fit to be a minister's wife. She should have recognized that. She should have turned down Austin's offer of marriage. She was totally lacking in the ability to perform the duties of a minister's wife.

The more she thought about it, the more depressed she became. She even had difficulty praying. Day after day she struggled on, and day by day her depression settled in more smugly around her until at times she felt she would surely suffocate.

I failed. I failed, her heart kept crying. And Anna feared that she could never be forgiven.

꩜ꃋ꩜ꃋ꩜ꃋ

A new baby girl joined their family on September sixth. Maggie was thrilled with her baby sister. They called her Rachael Ruth. The new little one lifted Anna's spirit to some extent, but the underlying heaviness did not leave her.

She prepared herself for another difficult winter. There would be daily laundry again. Anna would be glad to see the spring.

A missionary barrel came with a visit from the superintendent. It wasn't really a barrel; it was a box. A box filled with discarded clothes from people who could afford new ones. Anna breathed a sigh of relief. She had been wondering what she would do to outfit her two growing daughters.

Eagerly she began going through the clothes, anxious to find some material heavy enough to make Maggie a new winter coat. She had outgrown her other one and the days were getting colder.

But to Anna's disappointment, all the material in the box was light summer wear. There was nothing that would do for winter garments.

What can I do? wondered Anna. *I can't make something warm out of this material.*

Anna looked at her own winter coat. She could fare better than her young daughter against the cold. But her own coat was almost threadbare. She would really like to do something better than that for the little girl.

It wasn't until she was plumping up her pillow as she was retiring that the thought came to her. Feathers! Feathers were warm. She could use the lighter material and sew in a lining filled with feathers. That would give the coat lightness but plenty of warmth.

Anna could hardly sleep for her excitement. As soon as she had her breakfast dishes out of the way the next morning, she began to dismantle her pillow. She sewed throughout the day as she found the minutes. By suppertime the little garment was taking shape, and she laid it aside. She should have it ready for Sunday with no problem. And she still had feathers left over. She wasn't sure whether to make them into a cushion or save them in case she needed them for a warm garment for little Rachael.

That night as they prepared for bed, she noticed Austin's frown.

"Where's your pillow?" he asked Anna.

"I'm using the feathers for a coat lining," she admitted.

"A coat lining?"

"For Maggie. It will be warm, yet light. It's working well."

"But what will you do for a pillow?"

Anna shrugged aside his concern.

"It's probably easier on my neck to sleep flat," she said easily. "I have this bad habit of wadding the pillow up in a ball."

But Anna had a difficult time getting to sleep that night.

Chapter Twenty-two

Toughing It Out

Church conference time was approaching again, and Anna both looked forward to it and dreaded it at the same time. It would be good to see others who had the same desires—the same ministry as she and Austin. It would be nice to sit and chat with ladies who would understand her thoughts, her feelings. It would be nice to enjoy meals with a bit more variety. But Anna felt uncomfortable as she prepared their meager wardrobe for the coming event.

Her best dress was showing wear, besides being dreadfully out-of-date. Austin's good Sunday shirt was frayed at the collar and cuffs. The babies were short of suitable garments. She would need to rinse out clothing at the end of each day. Anna wished for another missionary barrel so that she might have some material for sewing.

Anna watched for the dray wagon each day, hoping for a freight delivery to her house but none came. Anna knew that she had little time left. She needed to take some action.

The first project was Austin's shirt. Carefully she removed the material from the back and sewed in its place a bleached portion of flour sacking. Then

Anna took the shirt material and fashioned new cuffs and a collar. When she had done the best she could do, she washed the garment; and after allowing the shirt to flutter in the soft afternoon breeze, she ironed it until the new collar and cuffs, stiffened with her flour starch, were without wrinkle. Anna looked at the result and felt a measure of satisfaction.

Austin spied the shirt as soon as he came in the door for supper.

"A new shirt! Where'd that come from? Just in time for Conference, too." He beamed his pleasure.

Anna was pleased.

Austin crossed to the shirt and let a finger trace over the stiff collar.

"Mama make it," piped up Maggie.

Austin laughed and scooped the little girl up into his arms.

"Your mama is a whiz," he informed her, "but she couldn't make a shirt."

"A-huh," said Maggie, emphatically nodding her head. "Mama did."

Anna felt her cheeks begin to flame. She felt almost deceitful. Austin was celebrating a new shirt—a new shirt with a flour-sack back. What would he say when he discovered the truth? Would he be too ashamed to wear it? He would be the only minister at Conference in such a circumstance. The other wives—

"I—I didn't make a new one," Anna quickly admitted, her eyes on the cutlery that she was placing near each place at the table. "I just—just made new cuffs and a collar."

There, it was out.

Austin reached out to lift a sleeve and study the cuff. "You did a great job," he commented.

Anna felt the air enter her lungs.

"Where did you get the material?" Austin asked innocently and Anna felt her cheeks flush again.

She turned and moved to the stove to dish up their supper.

"I—I had to—to take it from the back," she admitted, her head down, her face red.

"From the back?" Austin's voice, for the first time, was sounding concerned. He reached out and turned the shirt slightly.

"It's got a back," he said and Anna thought she heard relief in his voice.

Anger? Defiance? Defeat? Shame? Anna wasn't sure of the emotion that spurred her to answer sharply. "It has a back made of flour sacking." She almost spat out the words and the potato pot was set back down on the iron stove with a louder-than-usual bang. Anna could feel tears stinging her eyes and threatening to spill down her cheeks. She fought against them with all her strength.

But Austin seemed not to notice. He was still studying the shirt. Anna wondered what she would do if he refused to wear it. She could hardly undo the collar and cuffs and return them to the back of the shirt again.

"Ingenious," she heard Austin mutter. "Ingenious!"

Anna's head came up. Austin was still holding Maggie, but his hand was gently caressing the back of the shirt. There was a satisfied smile playing about his lips.

"Here I've been fretting about the state of my

collar—praying that somehow the Lord would provide a new shirt for Conference—and—and it was as simple as this."

Anna wasn't sure about the last statement. She had labored over the shirt all day. It had taken real effort to get the collar to sit just right and one cuff had nearly brought her to tears.

"You have a very special Mama," Austin was telling Maggie. "Did you know that?"

Maggie answered by nodding her head vigorously.

"You won't be able to take your coat off," Anna reminded Austin, feeling a need to put things back into proper perspective.

"That's no problem," he assured her.

"What if it gets too warm?"

"I'll just keep the vest on."

"No," said Anna, shaking her head, the shame of it staining her cheeks red, even at the thought. "Even the vest would not hide the shoulders. The difference will show."

"Then I'll leave my coat on," Austin went on, unperturbed.

"And if everyone else has his off?" pushed Anna.

Austin laughed. It seemed that facing reality was not as difficult for him as it had been for Anna.

"There is nothing wrong with being different," he said and he reached out to draw Anna to him. Maggie's little arm came out, too, making it a three-corner hug.

Anna let the tears slip out unattended. She was so thankful that her husband was appreciative rather than scornful of her efforts. How she longed to clothe her family properly. Surely a more skilled woman would have found a way—some way—to better care for their needs. She had never seen Reverend Angus look as shoddy as Austin was becoming. Mrs. Angus had seen to that.

Anna pushed aside the thoughts and concentrated on getting her family to the table for the simple meal. She wanted them fed before little Rachael awoke for her feeding.

It seemed that Austin would "get by" for another Conference. Anna's situation was not quite as easy to solve. She had no material for new garments. She didn't know what she should do.

"I—I was thinking," she said hesitantly as they ate their supper. "Maybe the girls and I should stay home this year."

Anna felt more than saw Austin's head come up.

"I thought you enjoyed Conference."

"I—I do," stammered Anna, and she could not keep her own eyes from lifting.

"Then why don't you want to go?" he asked candidly.

"Well, I—I just thought that it might be difficult this year with—with two little ones—and—and—"

But Anna knew she must be truthful.

"It will be hard," she said at last, "to find the proper clothing for all of us."

Austin's gaze lowered again. He looked troubled.

"I know," he said at last. "I haven't been a very good provider."

Anna's breath caught in her throat. She had not even considered that thought.

"Oh, but it's not your fault," she hurriedly responded, reaching out to clasp Austin's hand that rested on the table.

"It's been hard for you, Anna," Austin was saying. "I keep hoping that soon—soon we will have a big enough congregation that there will be enough in the offering plate to—to make things easier for you. But it just hasn't happened."

Austin pushed back slightly from the table and raised his hand to run his fingers through his hair.

"One convert—one struggling convert," Austin mused as though to himself. "That is hardly what one would call a thriving ministry."

"Austin, we don't seek converts to—to increase the offerings," Anna began softly and Austin swung to her, his eyes showing shock.

Then his shoulders slumped and he nodded his head.

"That was the way it sounded, wasn't it?" he admitted.

He let his hand run on down the back of his head and massage the base of his neck.

"That wasn't what I meant," he said wearily. "It's just—just—I feel like such a total failure. As a minister. As a husband and father."

Anna could not believe her ears. Had she done this? Had she made Austin feel a failure because of her inability to provide for the family?

"And—another Conference—when I have to stand before the whole body and say . . . one convert. One convert in four years of ministry."

Two, corrected Anna mentally. *Two converts. Have you forgotten Mrs. Cross, or are you crossing Matt off until he completes his probation?*

But Anna did not say the words. She was much

too busy trying to sort through the words of her husband. Anna had never heard Austin's voice so filled with anguish. She had never seen his shoulders so slumped, his body so drained of energy. She didn't know how or why, but somehow she knew that the fault was hers.

I couldn't even win Mrs. Paxton, her thoughts raced. *I couldn't even make her understand. No wonder Austin is unsuccessful in his ministry. He has chosen the wrong wife.*

Anna did not know what to say to her husband. How could she admit that she was the wrong choice for his life's partner without reminding him that he was the one who had made that choice?

She returned to her supper, but it was tasteless and unsavory. After trying a couple bites, she pushed back her plate. She could swallow no more.

Rachael cried. Anna was thankful for the interruption. She rose to her feet and hurried from the table.

The small body pressed warmly to her bosom was a measure of comfort to Anna. At least she was providing adequately for baby Rachael. She wasn't a total failure. And then her eyes fell on the simple, mended garment that had been washed so many times it was getting thin, and the tears begin to flow in spite of Anna's resolve. She had failed Rachael as well.

From the kitchen came the chatter of young Maggie and the soft voice of Austin as he responded. Her whole family had depended on her and she . . .

Just when Anna had reached her lowest spirits, Rachael turned from her nursing and looked up at her mother. A contented smile lit her blue eyes and her chubby cheeks dimpled as she smiled and cooed, her eyes intent on Anna's face.

"You don't know, do you? You don't realize that I've let you down. You think all that matters is that you're fed and diapered and—and loved."

The baby reached for the simple brooch on Anna's blouse. Her coos turned to bubble blowing.

Anna's vision blurred. She loved her babies. Loved her family. She did wish—did long to care for them better.

She lifted Rachael to coax up a burp and snuggled the tiny body against her shoulder. She needed the warmth, the comfort. She needed to feel that life had purpose—reason. That even in its confusion it made some kind of sense.

Rachael managed to get tiny fingers tangled in her mother's hair and soon had pins worked out and strands of hair falling about Anna's ears.

"You are sure making a mess of Mama," Anna softly scolded as she unwrapped the fingers, then drew them to her lips. Rachael responded with a squeal.

"Mama," called Maggie from the kitchen. "Mama, Papa an' me is all done."

"Did you clean up your plate?" asked Anna automatically and instantly remembered her own full plate of food.

"Yep, I did," answered Maggie and Anna heard Austin softly correct, "Yes, I did."

"Papa did, too," called Maggie, misinterpreting Austin's words. Anna heard Austin chuckle. It was a welcome sound. Anna hoped that his heaviness had passed. That he had been able to shake it better than she had.

Anna spent the next days mending, cleaning, pressing—and still her wardrobe was painfully inadequate. At last she broached the subject with Austin again. "I think that the girls and I will just stay home this year. By next year, perhaps Rachael will be trained and it will be much easier to attend."

Austin did not argue. He just answered softly, "Are you sure?"

Anna nodded. She hated to miss the opportunity of gathering with the other women. She hated to lose the chance for a good talk with Mrs. Angus. She hated to miss out on the tasty food, the laughter, the fellowship. But she did not want to disgrace her husband by appearing in worn garments, with two daughters dreadfully lacking in proper attire.

"I'll miss you," said Austin simply, but then the matter was dropped.

On the day of departure, Anna had Austin's suit brushed and pressed and waiting. It was showing wear in a number of spots, but at least it was clean. His shoes were polished until they glowed—and the worn toe did not show too much. Anna had used a little stove blackening under the polish.

Anna bade him a cheerful goodbye, straightening his tie and fixing the new collar so that it "set" properly. "I'll miss you," he said again as he embraced her.

Anna managed a smile. "It won't be long and you'll be home again," she assured him. "And remember, I want to know all the news. Keep notes if you have to."

He smiled. Anna expected a bit of teasing, but he just nodded his head in promise.

Austin kissed his little girls and turned to Anna one more time.

"If you need anything, call on Mr. Brady," he reminded her. Anna nodded.

"Bye, then."

"Bye," responded Anna, and then adding one last thought, she reached out and straightened an errant lapel, "Don't forget," she whispered to him, "don't take your coat off."

Chapter Twenty-three

News

"Where is Papa?" Maggie asked for what seemed to Anna to be the hundredth time.

"Papa is at Conference," she answered evenly.

"Why?"

"Because Papa had to go." Anna had tried to explain in fuller detail earlier, but the small girl had not understood. Now Anna shortened the exchange with a simple "Because."

"Why not me?" asked Maggie, pouting.

"Next time, perhaps," responded Anna.

"But I wanted this time," said Maggie, her chin lifting in her defiance. "I tell Papa, 'This time.'"

Anna nodded. She was busy folding laundered diapers and her thoughts were on the threadbare material rather than her daughter's disappointment at being left behind.

They are so thin, she mused to herself and then heard Maggie's "I not thin" as she stood to full height and puffed out her little chest.

"Not you," said Anna with a smile in spite of her troubled spirit. "Rachael's diapers. They are hardly worth putting on anymore."

Maggie reached out a hand to rub one of the folded diapers.

"If only I had some more material," continued Anna, though she knew that her little daughter had no idea what she was talking about, "I could sew Rachael some new didies."

"Maggie, too?"

"Maggie doesn't need didies. Maggie is a big girl." Anna was glad she had only one child needing diapering.

Rachael squealed and Maggie climbed from the kitchen chair where she had been watching her mother and ran to her baby sister. Anna scarcely heard the giggles and chatter.

The Indian mothers used to use soft moss, she was telling herself. *But I have no idea where one would find any.*

Anna's thoughts traveled on. *I wonder if there is anything else that might work. Feathers? No. Feathers would never do. There'd be no way to wash and dry them as needed. Surely—surely I have something around here I could spare so I could make new diapers.*

But Anna could think of nothing. She was already down to one sheet on her bed. She was short as it was of tea towels. They had no more bath towels or hand towels than they absolutely needed. All the usable materials from the last missionary barrel had already been used. There seemed to be nothing. Nothing.

Wool, thought Anna suddenly. *Wool might work.*

But Anna could think of no local farmers who raised sheep.

And then Anna thought of the quilt on their bed. "It has wool," she reasoned aloud. "I could take a bit from the edges."

Anna went to their bedroom and lifted a corner of their comforter. Carefully she examined it to determine where she could remove some of the batting without doing too much damage to the quilt. It might work. She removed the comforter and took it with her to the kitchen table. From this corner and that corner, and all along her side, she stole from the quilt, then restitched the seams.

With her little bunches of wool spread out before her, Anna began her task. She worked the wool with her fingers until she had it fluffy. Then she divided and shaped soft little piles. One by one she unfolded the worn diapers and inserted a piece of her precious wool in the center of each. The diapers took on a fluffier look, and Anna was sure they would be much better for Rachael. She wished she had more wool and then remembered that she didn't have any more diapers anyway. She was down to ten. That meant constant washings and struggles to get them dry on rainy or cool days. But she was managing and Rachael didn't seem any the worse for her lack.

"Don't bite," she heard Maggie cry suddenly, and the sharp comment was followed by a loud wail.

Anna turned from the table to hurry to her child.

"What happened?" she asked the crying Maggie.

"Rachael bite me," the girl managed through her tears.

"Babies don't have teeth," Anna reminded Maggie. She lifted the little girl, prepared to assure her that Rachael's bites were hardly worth all the fuss, but as she observed the finger that Maggie was holding out to her she did see a tiny mark.

"Whatever—?" she began but Maggie interrupted.

"She bite me," she maintained. "An' I didn't even bite her."

Rachael, who had been looking bewildered about all of the commotion, suddenly joined in the crying. Anna didn't know which daughter to try to comfort first.

"Rachael didn't mean to bite you," she began to explain to Maggie, but Maggie was in no mood to listen.

"She did," she argued. "She just put her mouth like this—right at me—and she just bite my finger like this—hard."

She demonstrated.

"I know," said Anna. "I know that she bit your finger, but she didn't mean to hurt you."

"Then why did she do it hard?" cried Maggie.

Anna eased herself to the floor and managed to lift both daughters onto her lap.

"Let Mama see," said Anna and Maggie held out her finger again. Yes, it did look like a little tooth mark.

"I didn't think Rachael had teeth—" she began.

Maggie interrupted through her tears, "Not teeth. I—I think Rachael has a needle."

Anna smiled. It may have felt like a needle to Maggie.

Anna turned her attention back to Rachael, who had stopped her crying and was studying her older sister with inquisitive eyes. The tears still glistened on the little round cheeks and clung to the long lashes, but Rachael seemed more amused than frightened now.

Anna tried again to calm Maggie and gradually the tears subsided.

"Now, let's check," Anna said to Maggie, a trace of excitement in her voice. "Remember that when Rachael was born, Mama told you the baby had no teeth. Well, maybe she has one now. That means our baby is starting to grow up."

Maggie still looked doubtful, though her crying had turned to sniffles.

"Let's check, shall we?" Anna asked again and shifted Maggie on her knee so that she could turn her attention to little Rachael.

Anna eased Rachael toward her and held her chin with one hand while she reached out a finger to check the little one's mouth. Anna already knew that Rachael hated being "checked" and she was ready for a protest.

But it was Maggie who responded. "Don't," she squealed, pushing Anna's finger away from the danger zone. "She bites!"

"I'll be careful," assured Anna and began the procedure again.

Yes, there was a little tooth. And yes, it was extremely sharp. Anna discovered just how sharp when the little tot champed down on her exploring finger. It was all that Anna could do to keep from responding with a little cry.

"Does she?" asked Maggie. "Does she got a tooth?"

Anna nodded. "Yes," she said. "Yes, she has a tooth all right."

Her finger still smarted.

"Will Papa be happy?" asked Maggie, wiping tears.

"Yes, Papa will be happy," answered Anna.

"Then he better come home—quick," said Maggie, "so we can tell him. Else he won't know nothin' at all 'bout Rachael's tooth."

Maggie gave her hand a little flourish and shrugged her tiny shoulders.

"Papa will be home tomorrow," Anna reminded her.

"Tomorrows are long times," observed Maggie.

"Not so long. Just one more sleep," replied Anna. But she admitted to herself that the four days of Austin's absence had seemed like a long time to her, too.

Anna lifted the two girls from her knees and got up from the floor rug.

"Should we tell him 'bout the tooth, or should we s'prise?" asked Maggie, all trace of tears now gone.

"Surprise, how?" asked Anna.

Maggie shrugged again but her eyes began to take on a glint. "Just let Rachael chew his thumb," she said simply. "Then he'll know."

Anna nodded. He'd know, all right. If Rachael chewed with the same voracity that she had just champed on her mother's finger.

"I think we'd better tell him," she said to Maggie and Maggie looked just a bit disappointed.

❧   ❧   ❧

The whole family was glad to see Austin arrive back home the following day. Maggie shouted her pleasure and at once pounced on Austin with scores of questions and animated tales of what had happened while he'd been gone. Rachael squealed and

waved chubby hands. Anna was the most re-
strained, but the most deeply affected. The house
had seemed so empty with Austin gone. It was the
first they had been separated since her one trip
home. She hadn't realized what a big piece of herself would be missing while he was away.

Throughout the afternoon, Austin thought of little bits of news to pass on to Anna. "Everyone
missed you," he informed her. "They sent their love.
Mrs. Angus said to be sure to greet you for her."

"How is she?" she asked Austin. Anna truly had
missed seeing the elderly woman with her gentle
ways.

"I think she looks a bit better than last year. I
guess retirement is giving her a bit of a chance to
rest."

Anna was pleased with the news.

Anna also heard that Milt Smith had needed an
emergency appendectomy. That Mrs. Buttle was expecting another child. That Reverend Willis was
having some serious eye problems. His wife now
had to read all the materials for his sermon preparation to him. Mrs. Giles was feeling much better
after her operation. The little Thomas boy had broken his leg in a fall from a swing. And Miss Small,
the college dean, was planning to be married after
forty years of spinsterhood.

"I saw Mrs. Whiting," went on Austin. "She is
the new Ladies' Aid president. She wondered if
there was anyone in our community who could use
another missionary barrel."

Anna held her breath.

"What did you say?" she finally asked when she

realized that Austin was not going to volunteer his answer.

"I told her that you were very good at making use of the items yourself and that with two growing girls you often sewed. She said she'd keep that in mind when they made up the barrel."

Anna felt a little prayer of thanks well from her heart.

"Did she say when they might send one?" she asked softly, trying hard not to get too impatient.

"She said they'd work on it next meeting," replied Austin, offhandedly.

Next meeting. Anna began to calculate. She should have some materials to work with well before another winter set in.

But Austin was speaking again.

"I must get to work on my Sunday sermon," he said to Anna. Then continued, "At least I feel that I have something to preach about again."

Anna did not understand the comment. But with Maggie clamoring for attention and Rachael wanting her supper, she did not have time to ask for an explanation.

☙ ☙ ☙

It wasn't until the girls had been tucked in bed for the night that Austin and Anna had an opportunity to really talk.

"I'm sorry you had to miss Conference," he told her. "I think that it was the best we've ever had."

"Best? How?" asked Anna.

"The most . . . encouraging. Refreshing. Challenging," responded Austin.

Anna looked at her husband. He did look refreshed. Again she felt sorrow that she had remained at home. She could have used some encouragement. Some refreshing.

"I admit," continued Austin, "that I was feeling rather down when I left. Defeated. I even wondered if I had really been called to the ministry, or if I had just assumed it on my own. I was seriously wondering if I should quit."

Anna's eyes widened.

"I mean," hurried on Austin, "my family have all been involved in one kind of ministry or another. I wondered if I just thought—well—that I should be, too. But—but nothing was happening—"

Austin stopped and rubbed his hand over his heavy thatch of hair and let his fingers curl around the nape of his neck.

Anna felt her chest tighten. It was her fault. Would Austin dare to say it?

"Reverend Morris, the evangelist, brought some powerful sermons," Austin went on, "and the sharing times yielded some strange discoveries."

Anna waited.

Austin let his hand drop from his neck and wrapped his long fingers around Anna's slim ones.

"Do you know that there were at least six other men who were sharing my same thoughts and feelings?"

"Six men thought you should quit the ministry?" asked Anna, her voice trembling.

Austin shook his head quickly. "No. No. Not me. They all thought *they* should quit. They thought that their ministry was ineffective. That they didn't have the ability to be servants."

Anna could not believe her ears. She might be Austin's problem, but she had nothing to do with the other men. Did she?

"And then Reverend Angus got up and spoke to us all, the tears running down his face as he spoke. 'Boys,' he said. It was strange to be called boys. 'Sons, don't let Satan use that lie to destroy your ministry,' he said. 'You see, it's his business to tell you that you are a failure. That you are letting God, the church, your families, yourselves down. Over the years of my ministry, he told me that many times, too. And I must admit, to my shame, that there were times when I believed him.' "

"He said that?" breathed Anna, her large eyes widening in incredulity.

Austin nodded. He lifted Anna's hand and held it in both of his own.

" 'God has called you—you are answerable only to Him,' Reverend Angus said. 'I don't believe God keeps the same set of statistics that we as the church find it necessary to keep. How many calls? How many conversions? How many baptisms? Those are kept for our records. Because we need some sort of accounting. But God's records are of another sort. How faithful to your calling? How concerned over lost souls? How willing to be obedient? How close a walk with Him? God doesn't care so much about statistics. But about faithfulness, commitment, obedience, devotion. That's what He wants to see. Growth. Personal growth.' "

Austin stopped to struggle with emotion. Anna held her breath. She wasn't sure what to say—how to respond.

"I've been on the wrong track, Anna," Austin

managed at last. "I think I've been more concerned about—about success than—than obedience."

Anna longed to argue, but she held her peace.

"God wants *me*—my love and devotion, even more than He wants my service," continued Austin. "I haven't really given Him that. I've been too busy worrying about getting converts."

"But converts—" began Anna.

"I know," Austin said quickly. "Converts are important. But because they are lost, they are loved. They are people for whom Christ died. For *His* sake—for *their* sakes—I need to give them that message of hope, but not for *my* sake, Anna. Not for my sake. Not for numbers in a book—or—or statistics to be sent to the superintendent."

Austin was trembling. Anna reached out to place her free hand on his arm.

"And I've been made to realize something else, too," went on Austin. "If I *never* have a convert in all of my years of ministry, I can still be faithful. I can still be obedient. You see, I don't make converts. I can't. I can only give the message. The Spirit must do the work of salvation—of conversion. There is no way that Austin Barker can save any man. Oh, I've known that all along, of course, but I haven't been acting like I did. I haven't been living like I did. I've been trying to carry the whole load myself. I've been thinking that it all depended on me. How well I preached. How much I prayed. How effective *I* was.

"Well, it doesn't, Anna. It *all* depends on the Lord. It has all along. My inadequacies, my lack of talent, of wisdom, that is no matter to the Lord. Scripture says that He can use the weak, the small, the inadequate. *Me*.

"I—I had no idea you were—were feeling those things," murmured Anna, clinging to Austin's hand. She didn't add, *I thought it was just me,* but she could have.

"I'm a man," said Austin, tears threatening. "I tried not to let it show. We bluff our way. To admit doubts would be to admit failure."

"But you haven't failed," argued Anna further. "We have a church instead of the schoolhouse. Mr. and Mrs. Cross have both become Christians. Several new people are attending—regularly. The neighborhood boys are no longer angry and troublesome. Some of them are even coming to church. You've not failed."

Austin patted her hand. Then he sniffed and chuckled softly. "Do you realize that all those things have come about through you?" he asked simply.

Anna could only stare open mouthed. "Oh, but that's not so," she hastened to argue. "You've done all the work on the new church."

"And who talked me into accepting the dingy old building?"

"But you—" began Anna. Austin was shaking his head.

"You explained to Matt—" Anna started again.

"Who made the first contact?"

"But—" Anna floundered.

Austin pulled her close and kissed her. He didn't argue further. Instead, he lifted her chin and looked deeply into her eyes. "I love you, Anna," he said simply. "If it wasn't for you, I would have given up long ago. God really knew what He was doing when He gave you to me." He kissed her on the nose.

Anna felt as if she were drowning in confusion.

Her strong, capable Austin had struggled with thoughts of depression and defeat. Austin, the one with the abilities, the talent, the intelligence, the training. He was leaning on her—the inadequate one. The one who had just finished eighth grade. The one who had no training for ministry. No wisdom in dealing with lost souls. No abilities in leadership. It didn't make any sense. Something was terribly scrambled. Anna felt weak with the unexpected, unwelcome discovery.

Chapter Twenty-four

Mrs. Angus

Daily Anna watched for the arrival of the missionary barrel. Each day she was disappointed. It was hard to be patient with fall approaching and so few proper garments on hand for her small daughters. She tried not to let her agitation show. Tried to pray and praise. But she felt her anxiety making her stomach knot.

"This is not faith," she scolded herself. "I know very well that God will provide our needs in plenty of time. Perhaps we will have a long, beautiful fall and I won't need the clothes for months yet."

And Anna determined that she would not fret but would wait for the Lord's provision whenever and however it should arrive.

But even her little bundles of wool stolen from her comforter were not doing a good job of keeping young Rachael dry. And Anna was terribly weary of the daily washing.

"It leaves me so little time for more important things," she often mourned inwardly.

And then there was the difficulty of drying the laundry. Anna liked to place her washing in the bright rays of the sun, but on more than one occasion she had almost lost her precious wool pads to the wind. On one such day she had chased fluffs of wool for two blocks down the street until she had been able to retrieve them. She had felt foolish and embarrassed as she raced along after the small handfuls of padding, but she had not dared to lose them. Rachael's dryness depended upon them, so Anna had hoisted her skirt and given chase. From then on she dried the small bits of wool indoors where the wind could not steal them away from her.

But it was hard finding drying space for even the small scraps. Anna tucked them everywhere. Under her kitchen stove, behind her kitchen stove, over her kitchen stove, and even in her warming oven. Maggie had finally been made to understand that she was not to play with the bits of wool, but Rachael, who was big enough to crawl but not old enough to understand, was often found with handfuls of the fluffy balls, bits and pieces on lips and tongue. Anna had to continually be on guard.

Anna knew that even wool would never get her baby through another winter. She also knew that she could not possibly pull more batting from her one quilt. It was quite thin in spots as it was. Anna tried to tell herself that she could sleep "cool." But she realized that in her sleep, she crowded Austin for warmth. That not only disturbed her rest but his as well. Anna knew that he needed his nights undisturbed if he was to profitably fill his days.

So Anna longed and looked for the missionary barrel. The family's wardrobe depended upon it.

And then one day as Anna worked over the tub of laundry, she heard a tap-tapping on the boards of the walk outside. Her first thought was of Mrs. Paxton, but just as quickly she dismissed it. Mrs.

Paxton was gone. It could not be her cane thumping its way down Anna's sidewalk.

Then Anna heard accompanying steps. Someone was coming to the house. Drying her hands on her apron, Anna moved toward the door, anticipating a knock.

When she opened the door, Anna could scarcely believe her eyes. There stood Reverend and Mrs. Angus!

"Oh my!" she cried. "I can't believe you are really here. Come in! Please, come in!"

Anna didn't know when she had been so pleased to receive company.

"The ladies had this big supply of clothing to come to you," explained Reverend Angus. "They were going to ship it, but my wife was anxious to see you, so we thought we'd bring it up ourselves."

Anna was doubly blessed. She beamed and motioned them into her kitchen. Mrs. Angus accepted the invitation and took the chair that Anna offered.

"I'll just go bring in those boxes," said Reverend Angus, "and then spend some time with your husband. Is he at the church?"

Anna nodded. "In his study," she responded. "He's working on Sunday's sermon."

"I hear he's a fine preacher," said Reverend Angus, seeming quite pleased with the fact, though Anna knew Austin would have liked to have seen more fruit from his efforts—even if it was now his intent to leave that aspect of his ministry with the Lord.

"I appreciate his sermons," Anna said simply.

Reverend Angus carried in four boxes of used clothing and stacked them in a corner of Anna's kitchen. Even in her excitement of welcoming her visitors, Anna was quite aware of their presence. She was anxious to open the boxes and sort through the contents. But that could wait. She was even more anxious to have a nice long visit with the older woman.

They talked of many things. Housekeeping. Babies. Fellow workers. World events. Anna had not enjoyed a visit so completely for some time.

"I was so disappointed when you didn't make Conference," the older woman said. "I decided that as soon as the opportunity presented itself, we'd just slip on up and see how things were going."

Anna toyed with her teacup. How were things going, she wondered? She didn't have a ready answer. Oh, certainly, on the surface things seemed to be fine. Austin was working hard and preaching faithfully. His sermons were well planned and expertly delivered. But the work had been hard. Had been without much result. Matt Cross had changed. Seemed to be making good progress. Mrs. Cross had asked for baptism. That was something to be thankful for.

But was it enough? Anna wondered. Should they have accomplished more in their time spent in the small town? Were people actually growing? Were the right people being contacted? In the right way? Certainly Austin was doing his best. He was faithful and obedient to his calling. What more could he do? The thoughts troubled Anna. If there was fault, if there was failure—and she feared that there was—then it was concerning her—her lack of ability and training for ministry. Anna felt the heaviness drag down her shoulders.

Mrs. Angus seemed to read the troubled look in her eyes.

"What was the real reason for your missing Conference?" Mrs. Angus prodded gently. "Have you been—been feeling just a mite angry with God?"

"Oh no!" said Anna quickly, jerking up her head. Never had she felt angry with God, only dreadfully inadequate and troubled.

"Good!" said Mrs. Angus. "I—I was just a bit concerned. You see many—I mean, a number of young minister's wives—well, they do feel a bit angry at times. I did."

Anna's eyes widened in surprise. It was hard to believe that Mrs. Angus had ever had such unholy thoughts and feelings.

"Well, sometimes, the hard times—well, they get to you. Especially when you have a hard time putting meals on the table. Clothes on the family. It's hard. Especially when others seem to fare much better."

Anna let her gaze drop. She had thought her problem an isolated one.

"Many of the young wives miss Conference because they are angry that they don't have new shoes or a new suit."

"I wasn't angry," Anna explained slowly. "I just didn't want to embarrass Austin."

Mrs. Angus nodded in understanding.

"And I didn't have enough clothes for the girls," went on Anna. "I would have needed to spend all my time doing laundry."

Mrs. Angus nodded again. "How are things now?" she asked simply.

"I've been waiting every day for the boxes," replied Anna honestly, her gaze drifting to the corner where they rested. "I do hope they will provide enough material for us to have new winter things. Maggie has outgrown everything she has and they are too worn to be of much use to Rachael. And my own things are dreadfully worn. Austin must be ashamed of me."

"Austin is so proud of you he nearly busts his buttons," Mrs. Angus responded quickly.

Anna managed a weak smile. It seemed so ironic.

"If—if that is true," she said hesitantly, "it is un-merited."

Mrs. Angus waited. Anna toyed with her wedding band. She didn't know what to say or how to say it. But she had to talk to someone. She had kept her pain, her doubts locked up inside for far too long.

"I—I was never cut out to be a minister's wife," she blurted out before she could change her mind. "I'm afraid that Austin made a dreadful mistake in marrying me. I—I have held back his ministry. I don't know how to do any of the things that—that minister's wives should know."

"And what things are those?" prompted Mrs. Angus softly.

"Well—how to lead the women. How to teach the children. How to—to—have a part in the music," stammered Anna.

Mrs. Angus waited for just a minute while Anna fidgeted.

"Well, let me see," the older woman said slowly. "I guess I wasn't much of a minister's wife either."

"Oh, but you were," Anna quickly defended, her

eyes widening. Anna had always seen the older woman as her role model.

"Well, I certainly wasn't gifted in leading the women. I did it because there was no one else to do it. I used to tremble with fear when I first started. I knew that there were many who could have done it much better than I."

Anna could scarcely believe her ears. She had never supposed that Mrs. Angus had ever felt nervous about her role.

"And I was never good with children. My husband used to chide me. Said I was far too exacting and far too impatient. I wanted them to sit still and listen, not wiggle and squirm."

This too was a surprise to Anna. She had idolized Mrs. Angus as her teacher, even though she remembered that the woman would abide no nonsense.

"And—did you ever hear me play an instrument?"

Anna shook her head.

"I tried to learn. Oh, I tried so hard when we were first married. I had no aptitude at all. I finally just gave it up, in tears. And I couldn't sing. I soon learned that it was best if I just sang softly—or even mouthed the words. I was afraid I would throw everyone else off key."

"Oh, but—"

"Now let's look at you," the woman went on. "The ladies give good reports about your leadership. Oh, don't look surprised. Those things do get back to Conference, you know. We have heard some very favorable comments."

"But I—I suffer each time I have to—"

"A little suffering just keeps us humble," said the woman. "That way we know that we must depend upon the Lord. And we also have heard that you relate very well to children. That you and your husband have managed to turn around a rather disreputable little gang of street rascals and have many of them attending services. That these same little scamps visit you regularly to feast on bread and jam. Right?"

"Well, yes—they come but—"

"And we've also heard that you presented an excellent Christmas program on your first attempt and have repeated it since, filling the church to overflowing each time."

"But that's because—they like to hear their offspring and so far we have found no one else to—"

"Exactly! That was why I took leadership, too. My dear, when my husband and I first went into the ministry, I was scared to death. I just knew that I didn't have the—the abilities that a minister's wife should have. I could have just curled up and let Satan defeat me. In fact, I would have had not a kind, elderly man in the church given me a little lecture. 'God does not ask you to be perfect,' he told me. 'Just willing. Just obedient. Just faithful in what you have been given.' After much prayer and trembling," the woman chuckled softly, "I realized he was right, so I took what I had—what I was—and I offered it to the Lord. I wasn't sure why He'd want it, or what He'd do with it, but I gave it to Him."

Anna felt her whole body tremble. She remembered the ministry of Mrs. Angus. She had done so much in the church—in the community. Everyone loved her. Everyone looked up to her. God had certainly used what the woman had given to Him. But she, Anna, knew that she didn't have anything to offer. She wasn't good at any of the things mentioned. There was just no one else to do them. So she managed to bungle her way through the tasks even though someone with ability could have accomplished so much more.

But Mrs. Angus didn't seem to understand. Anna decided not to argue further. In her heart she knew that the main reason for her feeling of inadequacy had not as yet been addressed. Dared she face it? Dared she admit her failure? Would the woman before her ever be able to forgive her sin? But Anna could no longer stand the weight of her burden. She lowered her gaze and blurted out her confession.

"I don't even know how . . . how to lead a person to the Lord."

Tears were running down her cheeks. Mrs. Angus reached out to clasp a trembling hand.

"We had a neighbor. Mrs. Paxton," Anna hurried on. "She was bitter and hurting. She gave us the church building. But—but I couldn't—couldn't even explain to her how—I couldn't make her understand. Me, the minister's wife. The only person that she would really talk to—and I couldn't say it right."

Anna lowered her face into her folded arms and let the sobs shake her shoulders. Mrs. Angus could only watch and pray and let the tears flow as she patted the young woman's shaking shoulder.

"Anna. Anna, listen to me," the woman said when the tears began to subside. "Do you suppose you are the only one who ever failed in such a way?

Do you think that everyone who is told the gospel story responds to it? Ministry would be so simple then. All we would have to do would be to proclaim the Good News. But it isn't like that. We are in a war, Anna. We have an enemy. The battle is long . . . and hard . . . and there are casualties. Satan does not easily let go of those he has blinded. And the will of the individual must also be reckoned with. The Spirit will force no one to a commitment. Only woo. Only draw him. The response is left up to the individual.

"Mrs. Paxton had a choice to make. You could not make the choice for her. You could only present the Truth to her. As hard as it is to bear, to let her go—unchanged into eternity—the choice was not yours, Anna. It was hers."

"But if I didn't make it clear," wept Anna.

"What did Mrs. Paxton say to your presentation of the Gospel?" asked Mrs. Angus.

"She said she had once been a believer but God had let her down. She said that she wanted nothing further to do with Him. That He had forsaken her in this life, so she didn't plan to have anything to do with Him in the next," Anna answered through her tears.

"So she *did* understand," responded Mrs. Angus. "She made the choice."

Anna thought about the statement. She guessed Mrs. Angus was right. Mrs. Paxton had understood. At least she had understood enough to turn her back on the forgiveness and love of a holy God.

"It's—it's terrible," said Anna, new tears beginning to fall. "How can someone—how can anyone—just choose to—to turn their back on mercy?"

"It's done all the time," responded Mrs. Angus, and her own shoulders sagged with the heaviness of the thought.

Anna cried for a minute longer, then lifted her head and blew her nose. She wiped her cheeks and sniffed away the sobs that still wanted to come. She would be waking her two little ones with her crying. She must get herself under control.

"It's so sad. So sad," she repeated. "Oh, I wish we could just pray—or—or push them into the Kingdom."

"That would not be in keeping with the will of the Father," said Mrs. Angus gently. "It was His will to give to each individual freedom of choice. Even He himself will not force them, though He longs for their salvation with a heart breaking with love and mercy."

The very thought nearly broke Anna's heart. And if she grieved, how must the Lord feel?

Rachael awoke. Anna wiped away her remaining tears and rose to get the baby.

The rest of the time together was spent in happier exchange. Mrs. Angus doted on the two small girls. Anna was happy to show them off.

"I just wish that my folks could see them," she lamented. "Mama would enjoy them so much. Austin has said that we might go home for a short visit sometime before winter sets in."

Anna thought again of the boxes of garments. Now she would be able to have her two daughters clothed properly for the trip.

"And Austin's folks plan to come for Christmas," Anna went on, the excitement filling her voice.

"Gramma's comin'," Maggie echoed, nodding her

head vigorously and jumping up and down. "A-huh. For Christmas. Next time."

Rachael squealed, knowing that something was making Maggie bounce with glee.

"That's wonderful," responded Mrs. Angus, reaching out to pull Maggie against her. "They will be so happy to see what a big girl you have become."

"An' Rachael, too," replied Maggie. "Rachael is getting big too."

"She certainly is," agreed Mrs. Angus, looking at young Rachael, who had pulled herself up at a kitchen chair. "She will soon be walking."

"Yeah," agreed Maggie and reached out a hand to Rachael. "Come on, Rachael. Walk," she coaxed. "I will help you."

Anna had to intervene. "No, Maggie. You aren't big enough to help Rachael walk. You might let her fall. You play with her on the floor." And Anna sat Rachael back down and gave her some kitchen spoons to play with. Maggie dropped down beside her little sister and offered her help.

"Here, Rachael," she said, "I'll show you how to make the best noise." And she did.

❧   ❧   ❧

As Reverend and Mrs. Angus took their leave, the older woman drew the younger toward her and whispered softly, "Remember, my dear. Your greatest and most important task is to *be you*. Austin chose you as his wife. For your love, your support. He has never been disappointed. You are an intelligent, gifted, sensitive person. That is enough. Don't try too hard to be all of those other things.

Just . . . just continue to be Anna. Give God *you*, Anna. *All* of you. Just as He made you."

Anna's eyes filled with tears.

Long after they had said their last goodbye and the door had closed, the words continued to ring in her ears, "Just continue to be Anna. Give God *you*, Anna. *All* of you. Just as He made you."

Chapter Twenty-five

Release

Anna spent hours in prayer in the days that followed. Even as she ripped seams and cut out new garments, her thoughts were on her spiritual walk. Through her talk with Mrs. Angus she had finally been able to forgive herself for failing Mrs. Paxton. Scripture after scripture came to her mind, helping her to realize that it was Mrs. Paxton who had ultimately made the decision whether to reject or accept Christ's atonement. Though Anna still grieved over the choice the woman had made, she realized there was no way that she could have forced a different decision.

But Anna still felt a heaviness about her lack of aptitude for the ministry. Surely she should have been more gifted for her role as Austin's helpmate.

Over and over she reviewed her conversation with Mrs. Angus. She had been shocked to learn that the woman had felt some of the same feelings of fear and frustration that she herself felt. She had always assumed that Mrs. Angus' poise had come so naturally. Had been God-given. That her willing and apt service had always been a part of the woman herself.

Now as Anna struggled, she tried to put things together in her mind.

First of all there was Austin. He had confessed to Anna his feelings of failure. What had he said? Something Reverend Angus had said about realizing that it was Satan's task to convince every individual that they were unworthy. A failure. Yes, agreed Anna at last. God says we are of worth. Satan tries to convince us that we are mere trash. Useless. Unusable. If he can accomplish that, then we give up. We do not even try to fulfill our God-given ministry to others.

Look at Moses, thought Anna. *"I can't do it." Think of Saul, hiding among the "stuff." And Jonah. He was so sure that the people wouldn't listen—that God was making a big mistake, that he tried to run away.*

It seemed so clear to Anna once she saw what Satan was attempting to do. She could now understand what Austin had tried to explain to her weeks earlier.

Then had come Austin's change of attitude after the recent Conference. His ministry had changed since his return. No, perhaps not his ministry. He was still doing things in much the same way. Still putting in long hours in sermon preparation. Still faithfully visiting his people. Still endeavoring to reach out to new families in the community. But his attitude was different. He worked as hard. Cared as much, but he didn't seem to have the heaviness that he had previously evidenced.

"I've turned the results over to the Lord," he had told Anna. "I realize that I can't change men's hearts. Only God, through His Spirit, can. So I must be faithful, but leave the results with Him. It's His work. His ministry. His power."

Anna was able to accept that truth as well. She knew that she in herself was capable of nothing of eternal value.

But Anna still struggled with who she was and what she had to offer for service. She was so void of abilities.

❧   ❧   ❧

I should take advantage of the quiet to read Austin's sermon, Anna said to herself.

The girls were having their afternoon nap. Anna had been busy at her sewing machine, turning out winter garments for her daughters and herself. The last missionary barrel had yielded more good material than she had dared to hope. Each day as she sewed, little prayers of thanks welled up within her. They would all be adequately cared for. There was even a suit that, when altered slightly, would be fine for Austin. And even beyond what she had dared to hope or pray for, two new Sunday shirts, one of them in almost-new condition. Anna felt dizzy with gratitude.

But now, the sewing must wait as she turned her attention to Austin's sermon while everything was quiet. He would be expecting her comments, perhaps at the supper hour.

So Anna settled herself at the kitchen table, sermon notes in hand.

The Sunday's message was on "Little Things." The title quickly caught Anna's attention.

"What is that in your hand, Moses?" was Austin's first question.

"Only a rod. A shepherd's rod. A simple 'tool.' A disposable 'tool.'"

Anna's eyes quickly went on down the page. God—the Almighty, all-powerful maker of heaven and earth—was asking for a simple shepherd's simple rod.

And, oh my. What He did with it!

Anna felt her heart beat with excitement as she watched how Austin skillfully and carefully developed the story and the lesson.

"'What do we have to feed the multitude?' Christ asked His disciples" was Austin's second point.

"Just a little boy's simple lunch."

But with that simple lunch, a multitude of people were fed, sustained, satisfied.

"What if the boy had held back what he had, knowing full well that it wouldn't be enough?" asked Austin. Anna could envision the hungry crowd, the crying babies, the staggering adults, struggling home through the heat and hills, weak and bereft.

Austin moved on to point three.

"Who will face the enemy—the Philistines?" was his next question.

"'We have here a lad . . . with a sling and five little stones,' was the answer."

"Did the people laugh? The enemy certainly did," Austin's sermon went on. "But not for long. 'I come to you in the name of the Lord,' cried David. Was that enough?"

Again, Anna felt her heart leap. She knew well the story. Could picture in her mind the stilling of the curling, sneering lips of Goliath.

"A little lad. His little sling. His tiny stones. What if he had been unwilling to use them for the Lord?" asked Austin. "What might the enemy have done to God's people?" Anna could easily imagine.

"What is it that you have to offer?" asked Austin's sermon notes. "Great things? Do you have great talents? Great abilities? Great goodness? If you do, you stand alone. If you do, God might not need you. He might not be able to use you—that is, until you realize that even your greatest abilities are small, so very small in comparison to all that God is. God does not ask for greatness—for strengths—even for goodness. No, our goodness is as filthy rags. Our talents and abilities are weak and feeble. 'Not by might, nor by power, but by my Spirit, saith the Lord,' according to Zechariah 4:6. And the apostle Paul in 2 Corinthians 12:9 added this, 'And he said unto me, My grace is sufficient for thee: for my strength is made perfect in weakness,' " quoted Austin.

"The secret is not in who we are—or what we are—but in our dedication to Him. In turning over all that we are—for His use—for His purpose. That is the secret. It is not whether we have been given ten talents, or five talents—or only one talent—but whether we are willing to release that talent into the hand of God—to let Him make use of that 'little thing' as He desires. He asks only for us—as He has created us. He decides who we are, what we are, what abilities, aptitudes, and gifts we have. We decide whether we are going to willingly give what we are—who we are—back to Him.

"It's simple really," concluded the sermon notes. "God made us. He loves us. He has provided for our redemption. He wants our love and devotion. He knows just what can be accomplished with the little that we have to offer Him. It all depends on whether we are willing to give Him free rein. Whether we are willing to say, 'Here is my *little,* Lord. Cast it down, break it up, hurl it out, as you see fit.' Only then will we be of use to the Master. Only then will we find fulfillment and contentment in life. Only then will we be given freedom—released to serve."

Anna's eyes were so filled with tears that she could scarcely read the script. "Released to serve." That was what she wanted. That was the freedom she wanted in her own life. She was tired of feeling weak and inadequate. She was weary of struggling on in her own strength—always falling short and feeling guilty. God had made her. He knew her shortcomings—her frailties. He was the only one who could take her 'little bit' and make it of any worth to anyone. Why did she continue to struggle to be more than she was? She knew that she needed His strength, His wisdom, His power. But for the first time, Anna realized that all she had to do was to *release* who she was—what she was—into the loving, trustworthy hand of God and accept what He had in mind for her. It was so easy. She didn't know why she hadn't realized it sooner.

She leaned her head on her arms and let the tears fall as her simple prayer lifted to her Father.

"Oh, God. I'm not much. I have so few—abilities. So few talents. Help me to accept myself, Anna, as you have made me. If you decided that I was—was *enough* with what you have given to me, then help me to accept it also. And what I am, I give back to you. *All* of me. My 'little bit.' Do with it as you see fit, Lord. Release me to freedom . . . for service."

A gentle and quiet peace began to fill Anna's being. She sensed deeply that God had heard her prayer. Her tears soon turned to tears of joy as the truth dawned, filling her being with warmth and peace. Her small, simple offering had been accepted by a holy God.

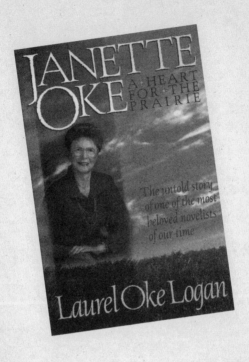

For those readers who enjoy Janette Oke's prairie fiction, here is the fascinating story of one of the most beloved novelists of our time. Written by her daughter, Janette's biography gives intimate glimpses into her life and heritage, and her fiction fans will find hints of characters and events that she has incorporated into her captivating stories.